ORIGINAL PRINTS

New Writing from Scottish Women

Introduction by Isobel Murray

POLYGON BOOKS

First published in Great Britain in 1985
by Polygon Books, Edinburgh.

© Copyright Individual Contributors
Introduction © Copyright Isobel Murray

ISBN 0 904919 98 6

Typeset in Palatino by
Edinburgh University Student Publications Board,
1 Buccleuch Place, Edinburgh, EH8 9LW.

Printed by Oxford University Press.

EDITOR'S NOTE

A year ago, I came across the writings of several literary critics, pointing out that women's writing is, and always has been, under-represented in literary anthologies and journals. When I looked for women's writing in Scottish publications, I found the same pattern.

Why should this be? Various critics have suggested that the definition of "literature" carries with it the idea that it should be about "serious life", and that women, in the eyes of men, do not lead sufficiently important lives to be worth writing about. Since most publishing houses and literary institutions are run by men, this seems to be a reasonable argument. But whatever the reason, even now when times are changing, women writers may recognise the status quo and be discouraged.

With a Scottish anthology specifically for new women writers, I wanted to give such women positive encouragement to write, and to give them the experience of sending their work to a publisher whose interest was guaranteed. I contacted dozens of writers, workshops and individual writers, and the enthusiastic response brought in hundreds of stories from women of all backgrounds from all over Scotland. It was clear from many of the letters I received that without my direct request for new women writers, few would have felt confident enough to send in their work.

I hope that *Original Prints* will be a starting point for other anthologies aimed at developing Scotland's resource of new writers of both sexes. In the meantime, I am delighted to be able to present some excellent new writers in this volume.

JULIE MILTON

CONTENTS

INTRODUCTION	*Isobel Murray*	1
THE GOLFER	*Linda McCann*	7
MISS MANGAN'S COMPLAINT	*Moira Burgess*	10
LUNCH	*Rosemary Mackay*	15
THE TEA-ROOM	*Jane Struth*	22
SHARING	*Wendy Stewart*	26
AGAPE	*Susan Campbell*	34
AFTERNOON NAP	*Joy Pitman*	37
OUR COUSIN CHRISSIE	*Elizabeth Case*	44
DIARY OF A SOCIALITE	*Joyce Begg*	49
IF FIND IT ALL A LITTLE BIT FRIGHTENING	*Linda McLean*	55
HAPPY FAMILIES	*Janette Walkinshaw*	57
SNAKES AND LADDERS	*Dilys Rose*	62
FELLOW TRAVELLERS	*Agnes Owens*	68
THINKING ABOUT MARRIAGE	*Rhiannon Williams*	75
MOONRUNNING	*Mary McCabe*	76
WALTER	*Anne Downie*	83
A FINISHED PICTURE	*Morelle Smith*	87
THE FOOD PARCEL	*Sheena Blackhall*	95
FOR BETTER OR ELSE	*Ellen McMillan*	98
MONSTERS	*Susan Campbell*	102
INCIDENT AT BAYONNE	*Jane Morris*	111
THE LETTER	*Iris Doyle*	116
THE EVIL PLANETS	*Jennifer Russell*	122
THE CHINA FACED DOLL	*Wilma Murray*	128
NOTES ON CONTRIBUTORS		136

INTRODUCTION

Isobel Murray

What you have in your hands now is a book of essays by writers you probably haven't come across before. Which shows you have a mind of your own and are open to new reading experiences. In the case of this volume, I am happy to say, your openness to the unknown is going to reward you, because it is a rich and varied collection of stories by some very individual new voices. I forecast you will look out for some of these names, eager to read more.

You may prefer indeed to start on them right away, leaving the introduction to be read as a postscript, if at all, and this is a procedure I rather recommend. But if you are staying with me, bear with a little recent personal history, an account of my reactions to the very notion of this volume, for I think there is matter of some interest here.

When Polygon asked me if I'd be interested in contributing an introduction to a collection of women's short stories, the stories in question were already selected: I had no hand in that, nor have I seen the many stories submitted and here omitted. My reasons for indicating the range and limitations of my responsibilities in this matter will become clear, and have nothing to do with lack of confidence in the selection, which I think is very good. No; what I am interested in first is my response to the Polygon invitation.

I was obviously faced with a couple of problems. I couldn't agree to contribute unless I thought the quality of the work was high enough: that was obviously problem number one. And inevitably I wondered about the constituencies the writers served: what *kind* of women writers? and would they be all of a kind? Was I facing a gaggle of frenetic feminists — or, worse, a rosy, cosy old-fashioned world of romances and happy endings? I was quite interested in the triteness of my own response, the stereotyped nature of my expectations. What hope for women in our society to be regarded without prejudice when after years of experience as critic and reviewer, a Scottish woman writer could have such qualms about Scottish women writers? The fact that my qualms were not wholly unjustified, that in Scotland as elsewhere we *do* have pockets of relatively frenzied feminists, and tracts of traditional moon-and-June romancers, only adds to the depression and confusion of the scene.

Anyway, the first thing was to read the stories. One reading was enough to answer problem number one: yes indeed, they were good enough. And it also dispelled the second problem: here was no one school of thought or interest-group, but a collection of writers who had in common at first sight only the facts that they were Scottish, and women, and writers.

How could I set the stories in context? I fixed on the series of annual volumes of short stories produced by the Scottish Arts Council in collaboration with Collins, of which twelve have been published since 1973. This series provides an interesting context. Its choice of contents is not the work of one editorial selector but a panel of three which regularly changes, and is apparently never identical two years running. The competition for inclusion is advertised nationally, and the volumes include authors old and new. It would be interesting to see how *Original Prints* compared with that valuable series, several of which I had reviewed appreciatively in their time.

I found the comparison disconcerting, however. Approaching with a volume of women's work, I saw the Collins series in a new light. Their twelve volumes have included a hundred and ninety stories, and of these forty-two are by women. That's not a great many — 22%, if my arithmetic serves me. Is there really such an inequality of talent parcelled out at birth to the two sexes? If not, what is the explanation? Do editors not expect to get valuable work from women? Or do women have similar expectations, fail to expect to produce valuable work, feel inadequate to enter such a national competition? Or do they expect their writing to be uncongenial to the Scottish Arts Council jury? Twenty-one women have had stories in the series — and sixty-two men (always assuming no misleading pseudonyms).

I wondered if these figures were less uneven than they appeared. The Scottish Arts Council jury has always intended, as Willis Pickard says, introducing the 1981 collection, "to carry the work of established and new writers alike." Perhaps a long process of conditioning and a male-dominated tradition had artificially but understandably produced more well-known male writers? But more laborious arithmetic indicated that there were a good number of established writers of both sexes represented, and when I put them respectfully aside I found the Collins series had published thirty-six "new-ish" women. There does seem to be a discrepancy, something more than the natural spread of talent. And it can hardly be a question of sex-prejudice in the jury, surely, when three of the volumes are introduced by women writers-cum-jurors, and these are among the volumes with the fewest female contributors.

Let us then just note the discrepancy, the unlikely imbalance, and see what conclusions we come to by and by. Women are not getting a big share of the space in the Collins series. This could be because they lack talent. Or experience and the expertise that comes with experience. Or time. Or confidence in their work. One reason surely has to be that our literary culture is still more male-dominated than we thought, even now. *Original Prints* has twenty-three female contributors, none of whom has had stories published in the Collins series; if this were a Collins volume only six of the authors would be women. But enough of the numbers game.

The brief introductions to the Collins series over the years tell us something about the aims of the series and the criteria of the judges, and sometimes quite a bit about the stories that don't get printed. The one thing they are all agreed on is that the outlets for short fiction continuously and sadly diminish. I haven't seen the stories Polygon is *not* publishing, but it is interesting and rather cheering that what the Collins writer-jurors — often themselves practitioners of the short story — find the most depressing defects are not very noticeable in *Original Prints*. Edwin Morgan, for example, in 1976, complains of "a distressing preponderance of the backward look." He gestures towards "reminiscence, nostalgia, kailyard melodrama . . . and stereotyped attitudes and expressions." I for one would happily acquit the present collection of over-indulgence in the backward look: on the whole its concerns seem to me preponderantly in the present, or even the future. Again Allan Massie, in 1980, rightly suggests that "one cannot but wonder about the health of a society whose writers deal most successfully with childhood and adolescence and tend to eschew adult life." And again it is interesting to skim *Original Prints* and find not only a due representation of childhood and adolescence (without over-indulgence), but a distinct preponderance of adult experience.

Anne Smith contributed the longest introduction yet to the 1984 Collins volume, and chose to do some plain-speaking to the unlucky and unselected competition entrants. She wrote of rough drafts of better stories, and verbal self-indulgence, of themes banal and repetitious and again of over-concentration on adolescence, and "so little evidence of life experience." I find most of the writing here tough and economical, and treatments of themes, however recognisable, that make them new — and above all I'd suggest that our writers give remarkable evidence of life experience, maturely rendered. Anne Smith was perhaps deliberately unfair, hoping to arouse women writers to indignation and response, when she said they seemed "on the whole, to lag behind the rest of the world in their preoccupations." And surely it was deliberately provocative of her to complain of the 1984 entries by women writers: "The big feminist issues such as wife-battering and pornography were completely ignored." Leaving aside the score on wife-battering (Collins 1: Polygon 1), is it appropriate to expect women writers to seize dutifully on "big feminist issues"? Is there an equivalent league of big "masculinst" issues?

My last experiment with the Collins series was to read through the forty-two stories by women they have published in the last twelve years to see how far, on an impressionistic, personal level, they reflected similar concerns and similar settings to those in *Original Prints*. On the whole the Collins women wrote of more colourful and surprising worlds. They dealt a little more often with wonderful happenings and imaginative characters — characters more likely to be exceptional or unusual than those of the Polygon women. Their worlds were more often middle class, or classless, and secure, and monied, with inevitable exceptions. And they wrote more of the past. The classless worlds of the Polygon writers are often so because the settings are fantastic or futuristic, and the recognisable class is most often the working class. Poverty and precariousness are more evident, and there are no colourful historical tales here. For all the crudity of this description, and the inappropriateness of labelling "middle-class" or "working-class" what is in both cases offered as something less blatant, more individually distinct, there seems to me a real difference here. The Polygon collection does not attempt to vie with the Collins stories: often they seem to complement them, seeming to offer new voices for a new constituency, opening up new areas in contemporary Scottish life and imagination.

And these voices are not offering too much for our comfort. They are adept at rendering the squalor and desolation of our inner cities, disturbed, angry or disoriented. This is not a question of anxious and unhappy *writers*, but rather a matter of writers holding the mirror up to the nature of our racked society in the eighties. The predominant

INTRODUCTION

after-taste is of disturbance, or menace.

And I don't think that if the stories were given to the reader
without authors' names it would ever occur to the unsuspicious
reader to think of an all-female production unit. Good fiction need
not betray its author's sex.

Finally, I'd like to shift my ground and briefly consider if these
stories say anything about the state of Scottish writing and its
principal preoccupations. In the first chapter of our *Ten Modern
Scottish Novels* (Aberdeen University Press, 1984), Bob Tait and I try
to make some very tentative generalizations about the ten novels we
have surveyed, published over five decades. I'd like now to use this
volume of·stories as a quick update of what we found there. This may
give us some indication of where Scottish fiction is moving.

In our ten novels from *A Scots Quair* to *Lanark* we found great and
heartening variety in techniques, social and geographical
backgrounds, historical periods covered. In *Original Prints* there is
still great variety in treatment, from the minutely observed realism of
smoking schoolgirls in a city graveyard to a persuasively inventive
Science Fiction-style forecast of tomorrow's world. There is less
variety of background; for whatever reason there is little evidence of
country life, and a concentration on urban townscapes, including
some of the most appalling devastated housing schemes. In *Ten
Modern Scottish Novels* we found a deal of preoccupation with social
bonds and their problems: we also found an affirmation of the
positive qualities of small and coherent communities, and even a
definable nostalgia for pre-industrial Scotland. If *Original Prints* is
any kind of indicator, in the mid-eighties there is more stress on the
bitter lack of social bonds or the impossibility of their holding, and
the affirmation — and the nostalgia — have been put aside. History
has been put aside too.

We noticed a rich variety of comic techniques and modes which
lightened the often bleak subject matter of our novelists: in these
short stories the comic impulse is absent, or considerably subdued,
although subdued to good effect in a new view of the Cinderella
story or the portrait of a self-deceiving Catholic spinster. We found a
series of analyses of the continuing psychological effects of
Calvinism on Scotland, and some expressions of wider, positive
spirituality: I don't find them here. I do find the same class division,
noted without protest, and a similar presentation of communities
ridden with conflicts. Male/female relationships here, as in our ten
novels, are seen as generally unsatisfactory.

In all, we found that "most of our novelists find very little to cheer
about." As I've said, this collection is too various to generalize about

5

too blandly and frequently, but here, as in our novels, all too often "it's a grim old world on both social and personal levels." One collection of stories from twenty-three people can at most be a straw in the wind, and I've suggested that what we have here may be a new constituency rather than a change in the tradition; but on this evidence, if Scottish fiction has moved in the last few years, arguably it has become less Scottish. Gone are our national obsessions with the glorious failure of the past, our rage against Calvinism, our justified sinners and lost Edens. Gone too perhaps the self-consciously Scottish stance.

The next question may be whether Scots, and in particular new Scottish writers, are losing their sense of particular nationality and national identity, and merging into an unhappy, urban world of characterless unease and disturbance. Is it happening, and does it matter?

THE GOLFER

Linda McCann

The matchsticks sailed a triangular route in the stale beer, turning sharply at each tide as frothing pint tumblers were replaced on the small round table. There was a sudden draught as the doors swung shut behind a huddled man who clutched a white plastic bag and looked around as though he had been expected for some time. "Right! Okay! A tenner fur the lot!" He waited confidently, as if that was his final offer, take it or leave it. The eyes which had looked up to see who had come in, now lowered as the men exchanged ironic grunts, sharing him as a private joke they had all heard many times. "Ah'm tellin' yeze — two pound fifty ther up the road. Each!" His eyebrows raised slightly in great discretion and he looked towards the bar as he held the bag open, passing it under the nearest noses. There was a whiff of earth and grass, perhaps with a suggestion of manure.

An interested woman sitting just too far off to see, leaned across and asked "Whit's that?'

"Ach, that's The Golfer," answered one of the more resident regulars. There was a burst of mocking laughter from someone who emerged from the toilet, zipping up his fly.

"Aw Jesus Christ, look who it is! Ye're gettin' nuthin' in here the day. Goin'. Beat it — get tae fuck — oap — sorry hen." He went back to his pint and forgot he'd seen him. The Golfer just stood and smiled.

A guy rolling a joint on the shelf beneath his table, looked up and across at the woman who had spoken, and she looked back at him through her raised glass, made small by the gold sovereigns on the fingers that held it. He asked casually, "Have you got any wee lassies?"

"How?" she replied, frowning suspiciously.

"Are they needin' any school skirts?"

The woman had a grand-daughter due to start school the following week. "Aye. Whit kinna skirts?"

"School skirts." The cigarette papers were not rolling as neatly as they had been. "Here," he said to the person sitting next to him, "Gonny finish this." He slid it round to the next space between the table legs and picked up his latest pernod and blackcurrant, one of the three drinks that were now waiting for him. He drank it in one and then someone tapped him on the shoulder and gave him his turn of the joint that was currently circulating. He took a few cool puffs before passing it on and pulling up the squashed parcel he'd been sitting on. The woman's friend now returned from her long visit to the ladies'. She was accompanied by a cloud of choking hairspray, and when she drank, her lips left a bright pink print on her glass.

By this time, The Golfer had bid himself down to two pounds fifty. A voice asked "Is that golf balls you've goat Tam?"

"Aye," he answered, swinging round, "Three-fifty fur the lot."

"Let's see an example of one." The specimen golf ball had a black crack and stamped on it was "Stolen from Sandy Meechan." "Aye," considered the potential customer, "I like a spot of the old golf efter luncheon, right enough."

The Golfer's wellies had left a trail of mud on the floor and there was a square of darker blue on the back of his denims where a pocket had once been. He snatched the ball back and said "Right — Ah've nae mer time" and, turning to the barman, he said "Just geeza canna lager fur them then."

Golf balls were forgotten in the sudden roar of cheering when the skirt salesman appeared from the gents', modelling one of his skirts. He was wiggling in increasing circles and doing little coy flicks with the back of the skirt, giving cheeky glimpses of a bare bum. Each flick was greeted with great approval, and soon his bird-thin legs were kicking as he pranced to the loud chorus of "Big Spender", holding onto the front of the skirt with both hands and giving it big triumphant wheechs, revealing all. The skirts were soon sold, and after a few more of the drinks that were bought for him he was sound asleep, propped in the corner in a heap of muddy sawdust, his trousers back on but his shoes missing and most of his toes through the holes in his socks.

The barman shook his head and put it all down to the funny

cigarettes he was always pretending not to notice. The woman said to her friend, "Whit's that smell?"

"Aye," said the man nearest to her, "Heh, who's dayin' that? Huv you stood oan somethin'?" He continued to loudly and accusingly express his disgust, while the barman calmly unhooked the gate of the bar and stepped down. An old tramp had wandered in and had dirtied a brown pattern on the back of his beige trousers.

"Right. Oot ye go," said the barman, who had seen him coming in and now turned him round and guided him right out again.

"Ach, it's him," someone said, adding "Heh, it's a good joab he didnae hear you ther Jimmy — he might huv sat oan ye."

"Right — you an' a'," said the barman, turning to The Golfer, "Oot."

The Golfer left after cheerfully raising his hand and shouting "Right. See yeze!"

As the doors battered shut again, someone asked "Whit dae ye make o' him way they golf baws?"

"Aye, Ah know," said his friend, "Ah bet there's plenty o' magic mushrooms in that golf course an' a', if ye looked. A bloody fortune he'd make in here way them."

"Aye," said the other, "Ah kin jist picture him in ther at night, trampin' oan millyins o' magic mushrooms an' sayin' tae eezsel 'Ah, a golf ball!'"

Long after the pubs were shut, The Golfer was still wandering the streets, stopping the occasional dressed-up passer-by coming from the dancing, and asking him for a loan of ten pence. There was some dried blood smeared between his nose and upper lip, as someone had mugged him for his bag of golf balls, thinking it was a carry-out. He strolled up Byres Road, and he watched the nightshift men in black felt jackets, sweeping away the leftovers of another day. He looked for some time in a shop window, at the neat rows of assorted styles, all waiting for different feet, different smells.

MISS MANGAN'S COMPLAINT

Moira Burgess

Thursday morning, half-way through the parish mission; Miss Mangan slipped breathless into a side pew and bowed her repentant head. Dear Lord, I am heartily sorry that I was nearly late, but it wasn't my fault was it, those wild children stravaiging all over the pavement, and their mothers as bad in their wee short skirts, and some of them bulging out in dungarees though they're far gone expecting, dear Lord forgive me for thinking about such things.

She drew her rosary beads from their scuffed leather purse and set her fingers on the first cool smooth curve; but already it was time to stand up for the priest coming in. It was the young one, oh, he said mass beautifully, with a light in his dark eyes as if it was all still fresh and new. His thin face was tanned from the sun and wind of the lovely autumn weather. He smiled and invited them to sit down, waiting courteously for a few latecomers to settle.

Two rows ahead of Miss Mangan the red-haired young man she saw every moning genuflected and slid into a pew, remaining on his knees. His head was bent over his clasped hands: his hair was long enough to have a bit of soft curl at the ends. He had the right stuff in him, Miss Mangan knew. On Tuesday there had been no server, and at a murmur from the priest he had gone on to the altar, just as he was in his shabby bomber jacket and jeans. Ten o'clock mass every day; he must be unemployed surely, though his long hands, gravely assured in the ritual moves, weren't the hands of a working man. He would be a varsity graduate no doubt, and finding it hard to get work as the common scruff, which was a sin and a shame. Best of all was to see him kneeling. There was something about a man kneeling, his strength humbled though you knew it was there —

There was a server today, a scrubby schoolboy in old tennis shoes; and now the priest's thick-lashed dark gaze almost seemed to be resting on Miss Mangan. Dear Lord forgive me for these wandering thoughts. She concentrated on the young priest's smooth face. He smiled round the church again and spoke his opening words: how good it was that they didn't let the business of everyday life distract them from paying attention to God.

Well, I don't, thought Miss Mangan, not like some. She had taken care to have breakfast early, punctiliously washing and putting away her plate, cup, saucer and spoon; and then to be held up, nearly late, because of the schoolchildren and their foolish mothers! The children streeling back from the chapel after their mission talk — two neat lines had been the rule in her day — and some bad little one at the front seeing his mother on her way to the shops. And when one stopped to wave, wouldn't they all follow suit, and wouldn't you know the big ones at the back would fall over them? The mothers not one bit put out, waving and laughing too; you couldn't get along the pavement on your lawful business for children and push-chairs and bulging — O God *forgive* me . . . And turning away quite cheerful to buy their story magazines and their cigarettes. Not much sign of them going to the mission.

Miss Mangan stood up for the gospel, reverently signing brow, lips and heart. No, they weren't in the chapel, those hussies, but she was, not a day missed so far. She listened carefully to the young priest's poured-honey Irish voice; his front teeth were very slightly too large, like a schoolboy's, and occasionally showed endearingly as he spoke. His hands were bony like a schoolboy's, but strong and gentle as he turned the sacred page.

And there in the middle of the gospel itself, didn't two young mothers with three toddlers between them come trolloping up the aisle! They planked themselves down immediately in front of Miss Mangan, like a tinker's camp with their sweeties and toys and paper hankies, the noses being wiped, the smallest child kneeling backwards on the bench to peer unnervingly into Miss Mangan's face. And the priest having to pause in his reading, even smiling a little at the wriggling weans! Father Riordan would have scowled; once he even made a remark from the pulpit, not that it did much good, still they would come rolling in with three under five and another —

Dear Lord, I'm thoroughly distracted today, but really it's no wonder, that carry-on in the street and now this crew in front. Half the mass over and I've hardly had a chance to hear the priest. Miss Mangan sat down, moving slightly sideways to avoid the small dribbling face hung over the back of the pew.

She couldn't now see the red-haired young man. She had to settle for a view of him after communion, coming back down the aisle, arms folded, chewing slightly. He couldn't be blamed, they didn't tell them at school nowadays not to chew. He rather needed a shave. His eyes flickered round the church as he turned into his seat. What was in his mind? You knew what ought to be in a person's mind as they came down from communion, but there could be distractions for the most devout. O Lord, Miss Mangan correctly added to her post-communion prayers, let me not be a distraction for this man. I wonder who he was looking for, though?

The mission talk after mass this morning was on Purity. You would think the priest had read her mind. He looked gravely round his ten o'clock congregation, pensioners, the young mums, the red-haired young man and Miss Mangan; he cleared his throat, addressed himself to a pillar, and spoke of holy purity.

A suggestion of red touched his high cheekbones. He spoke of purity in thought, word and deed. He blamed factors in modern society; but to protect our young people was there not the blessing of a good Catholic home and the example of a good mother? (That's one for them, Miss Mangan thought.) He touched on the religious life, and his dark eyes glowed with joy; many a poor soul might envy him, Miss Mangan thought, safe in harbour with all temptations past.

And then he spoke, as they always did, of chastity in married life.

Miss Mangan stared yet more intently at his eager, explaining face. Maybe this time he would make it clear. They always mentioned it, but they always skirted round what she wanted to know. How could you be chaste, how could you even look the world in the eye, and do — and do —

In a terrible moment, vivid as truth, she saw the young priest standing there on the steps of the altar, tall and broad-shouldered and narrow-hipped and naked like a bridegroom in his power.

She covered her horrified face with her hands as the heat ran up her body and the sweat pricked under her breasts. Oh horrible, such thoughts at mass, and about a priest too! She heard no more of the talk. She prayed no one had seen her scarlet face. Please God no-one had guessed her thoughts. She prayed, though bleakly she knew it impossible, that not even God guessed those.

By the end of mass she was calm again. She would forget that dreadful moment. You weren't responsible for your thoughts, after all, it wasn't even matter for confession. She imposed her own penance by not allowing herself to look after the young priest as he went into the sacristy; her mind might have followed him as he began to disrobe, and then — Instead she hurried out of church just behind the red-haired young man, who was hurrying too. Perhaps he had a job after all, or maybe a chance of one, an interview; as she blessed herself Miss Mangan prayed for his success.

But there at the corner of the street was the reason for his haste.

At least she had a wedding ring, but she was in those disgusting dungarees, round and smooth as an egg. The young man kissed her on the lips, practically outside the chapel as they were.

"How's it comin' then?" he said.

"Thirty-five weeks," she said, "daein' great," and beamed as if it was the cleverest thing in the world.

They linked arms and strolled along past the school railings, which unfortunately was Miss Mangan's way too. It was the morning interval and the children were out in the sun, screaming fit to split the sky, galloping and jumping and doing karate kicks. Two little girls ran down to the gate to speak to the young man and his wife. They were about ten years old; their skirts were tucked up into their knickers and their long thin legs twinkled as they ran, pretending to be Olympic athletes, down the school path.

"End o' next month," said the young man to one of the girls, maybe his sister from her red hair, and she jumped up and down with excitement. Miss Mangan felt sick. To speak of that to a child! She hesitated, wondering if it would be too obvious to march past them and go on her way. She had left the decision too late; she stopped and stared fixedly over the railings, as if at some child she knew.

"So whit's the game the day?" said the pregnant young wife, creamily secure in her near-motherhood.

"Chinks," said the little girls together, "look!"

Miss Mangan looked across the playground at the ten-year-old girls. Over ropes made of knotted rubber bands they were jumping and hopping and skipping in a prearranged sequence of moves. The ropes were raised higher after every new move, so that as a climax they had to fling themselves over in handstands. They all had their skirts tucked up. Their hair, escaping from ribbons and clasps, whipped about their tanned smooth young faces. Their lithe bare legs ran and hopped and scissor-kicked and wheeled through the sunny air.

"See an' no' miss your shot, well," said the young man. The girls ran off shouting, and the man and the woman moved away. Miss

Mangan waited a nervous moment before following. Even going along the street, they were close as one flesh. As they walked, the red-haired young man put his hand down behind his wife, and, grinning, he —

Miss Mangan turned away, feeling the heat surge darkly up her neck; she stared fiercely over the playground, but she saw only that vulgar possessive caress, and the young woman's laughing face upturned. Her eyes cleared. She was looking at the game of Chinks, the ten-year-olds running and jumping in the sunny morning, the pale curves of their long legs flying heedless for all to see, young muscled thighs, naked to the very hips. Miss Mangan pressed her lips together and hurried up the path into the school.

Next morning after mass it was as before: the red-haired young man, unshaven and hot-eyed, kissing his breeding wife on the steps of the chapel itself. Miss Mangan walked primly behind them as far as the school playground, where the ten-year-old girls were slouching about, nagging at one another, calling raucously to the boys.

"Nae Chinks the day?" the young man asked when the two girls came down to the gate.

The little girls' faces twisted in disgust. "Miss Leary says somebody complained aboot us," they said. "We're no' tae play Chinks, she says. We're big girls now, she says. Handstands is for the gym."

"An' we hud oor skirts tucked in!" the smaller one cried.

Miss Mangan hurried on without hearing the reply. Fish for lunch today, though not many bothered now. She breathed with satisfaction the sunny afternoon air. Only one more day and she would have made the mission perfectly; and struck a blow for purity besides. Her right hand found the rosary beads in her coat pocket and her fingers moved prayerfully over their pregnant curves.

LUNCH

Helen Florence

As Annie walked down the corridor towards the Toilets:Girls, a swinging glass door blew open and an icy blast clutched her long, thin legs. She dug her hands deep into her pockets and hunched her meagre shoulders inside the threadbare school blazer. In one curled palm she rolled her dinner-money; in the other, she clasped a half-empty cardboard sheet of matches. She hadn't had a cigarette since the early-morning bus and her mind and body craved past the mince-pie to the first long, shuddering draw.

She could see Kirsty and Eileen through the glass corridor, huddling outside the toilet-block door. Eileen's long hair was lashed to her face, but her short, fat legs and built-up shoes were unmistakable. Kirsty, her skirt barely visible beneath the bottom edge of her blazer, was in typical knock-kneed stance, head jutting forward. Her hair, styled expensively in an inverted W emphasised the shortness of her neck. Annie got a quick picture of her, in motion, blazer pulled tight across her ample rump, feet slapping down pigeon-toed, and was reminded of a chimpanzee. She sniggered, mouth closed, and the snot shot down from her sinuses into her nostrils. She sniffed hard and pushed through the doors.

Kirsty saw her first and turned to move off. Eileen, nearly blind with hair, opened her mouth to speak, and Annie elbowed her as she passed.

"Aye. OK.", said Eileen and stepped after them.

They turned the corner towards the Toilet:Boys, making the necessary detour round the open door to avoid the stench which, like a solid wall, always reached the same distance across the playground. They went out the back gate.

Nudging each other as they moved, they walked close together, in an effort to shut out the biting wind. It wasn't raining, but the low sky and tall buildings seemed to absorb whatever light there was. It had been overcast all day and soon darkness would fall.

They were almost at the Café when Eileen said, "Yous gan doon Patagonian?"

Kirsty and Annie stopped and looked at her. She stared back at them. The cold had drawn tears and the mascara was beginning to run at the corners of her eyes. Her face was purple-patched. The wind whipped her hair round and she was lost.

"I've got none," said Annie.

"I've got," said Kirsty, her face pained. She always had cigarettes, but was loath to admit it.

"Come on, then," said Eileen and started across the street, letting the change in direction return her sight.

Patagonia was a short close with steep steps just off the main street, dangerously near the school except that no-one bothered to look down it, since the restaurant next door stacked its teeming dustbins there. They edged past these and walked down to the cobbled floor. Annie glanced back to the top of the steps and was reassured by the sight of a disembodied head moving past, oblivious.

Eileen dug two fingers into her top pocket and produced a concertina'd and bent tabby. Annie could smell it from where she stood.

"Christ," she said. "I've stepped on bigger ones."

Eileen grinned at her.

"Beggars canna be choosers. Gie's a light."

Annie fished in her pocket for matches. Kirsty was holding a ten-packet close to her chest, the cardboard top held upright, so that they couldn't see how many she had. She slipped a whole cigarette between pouting lips, and the packet disappeared.

Annie was salivating and her stomach was beginning to churn. She cupped the flaring match round the end of Eileen's tabby as Kirsty pushed her head forward. She held the match for her, turning in time to see Eileen take a last pull and drop the end on the ground. Annie trod it out. She looked at Kirsty who stared back. Eileen watched. Kirsty's mouth twisted into her version of a smile as she held out the cigarette. Eileen reached but Annie grabbed it.

"For God's sake," said Kirsty.

Annie drew deep on the cigarette till the end glowed brightly and passed it to Eileen. She did the same and passed it on to Kirsty, who closed her large, wet lips on the filter. Annie winced.

"I'm starving," said Eileen.

Annie reached for the cigarette. It was almost finished, the tip as long as the cigarette itself, pointed like a spear. Annie put the filter to her lips and drew. It was red-hot and tasteless. She hated fags when they were like that, spoiled.

She made to pass it on, but Kirsty said, "It's mine. I'll have the last drag."

Eileen gaped.

"You'd one of your own," snapped Kirsty. She drew slowly, then dropped the end and scraped her sole across it. Annie looked down. The paper was split and what tobacco had remained speckled the stones. Kirsty did everything in a clumsy, ugly way.

"Clarty bitch," thought Annie as they began to climb back up the steps.

The Café, long and narrow, was packed as usual. The three girls pushed past the wee ones at the sweetie counter to the hot-pie stand. The place was badly lit, but warm and smelling of cooked food. Downstairs, they could see workmen sitting at tables spooning soup into wide mouths. The owner gave them a big smile. He was a tall, immaculately-groomed, middle-aged man, ludicrously out of place.

"What can I do for you, Ladies?" he said, over the heads of two boys.

Kirsty's large breasts and swollen lips were an advantage wherever they went.

"Three hot pies," said Kirsty and fluttered her eyelids. He tried to serve the pies into paper bags without taking his eyes of Kirsty's front. He was improving, but his confidence was in advance of his technique. He let the last one fall on the counter.

"I'll give you half-price for that one," sneered Annie.

Being so thin, she looked three years younger than her friends. He ignored her, slipping the pie into a bag and pushing them across the counter towards the girls.

"Anything else, Ladies? he smiled at Kirsty.

"I'm needing two fags," said Eileen, quietly.

"I'll have the same," said Annie.

He reached behind him for a ten-packet lying open on the shelf and laid four cigarettes on the counter.

"And you, my dearie?" he smiled into Kirsty's eyes.

She cast them demurely down.

"I'll have a doughring, pleath," she lisped.

Annie grinned round at Eileen, who was concentrating on easing

17

the cigarettes into her top pocket. She watched the doughring being handed over.

"Greedy bitch," she thought.

They paid and left.

There was a brief jockeying for position as they moved off. The one in the middle got better protection from the wind and Kirsty, the heaviest, usually landed there. They walked with elbows crammed against their ribs, both hands holding the hot pie. They passed two women teachers on their way to a restaurant lunch. In warm coats, they appeared little affected by the cold. Eileen and Kirsty pointedly looked away as the teachers passed, but Annie caught the eye of one of them and nodded.

They headed past the school and round to the graveyard. It was the oldest in town, with ancient gravestones rubbed smoothly illegible. Large, gnarled trees drooped over sections of it, creating bowers and semi-private areas used by couples and exhausted old folk in the summer. Now, with the trees stripped bare, human forms could be made out here and there.

The girls trudged to the centre area which, because of the lay-out of the paths and crush of gravestones, afforded the best concealment. Eileen and Kirsty sat down on a horizontal gravestone turned moss-green with age. Annie leaned against a nearby upright, preferring shelter to a seat. She scooped the pie out of the bag, wrapping it around with the paper. She concentrated her attention on it, shutting out all other impressions. Her tongue swimming in saliva, she took a deep bite and closed her eyes. She suppressed an image of Eileen eating, strands of hair in amongst her pie, and opened her eyes to the view.

She liked the sombre greys and dark earth of the place, preferring now to the summer, when the leaf-slanted sunlight irritated her. The location of the graveyard acted as a wind tunnel and sun-bathing was better elsewhere. She closed her eyes and bit deep again. She could feel a trickle of grease ease itself from the corner of her mouth and she wiped it on the edge of the bag. She looked at the pie. Two more bites and it would be gone. Her toes were so cold that they were aching. Eileen's eyes were two black patches on a blue background, her lips mauve. Kirsty's face seemed to shrink with cold, her skin pulling taut. Her lips grew and her eyes bulged under a heavy, dark fringe.

Kirsty finished her pie and tossed the crumpled bag down, feeling for her cigarette packet. Annie took the last bite of her pie and began to smile. She waited until Kirsty's packet was open, then produced her matches.

"Light?" she said.

LUNCH

She stepped forward, twisting her head to see.

"Got enough, have you?" she said.

Kirsty flattened the packet against her chest and glared. Annie hadn't managed to see how many there were, but beamed at Kirsty.

"I'm fine, ta," said Kirsty and put a cigarette in her mouth. Annie waited for Eileen, then struck a match, cupping a hand round it. Eileen was too quick and knocked it out. Kirsty snatched the matches.

"Let me."

The wind took the first, but she lit up with the second, leaving two unspent.

"Anybody else got spunks?"

No-one answered. Eileen and Annie lit theirs off Kirsty's and Annie returned to her gravestone. She smiled at the whole cigarette in her hand.

"Ah'm gan back efter this. It's ower bloody cal'," said Eileen. Kirsty brought out the doughring and took a big bite, eyes wide. Annie watched her, becoming aware that she was wearing an odd expression. She wasn't chewing properly, seeming to have difficulty with the lump in her mouth. Eileen was staring straight ahead, blankly. Annie turned her head to see, then heard the growling.

A small, ageing man in a dark suit was shuffling towards them in the gloom and seemed to be punching himself in the groin. The sounds he was making began to sort themselves out into: "Bitches. Dirty bitches."

Annie realised what was happening and began to laugh quietly. She turned back to look at Kirsty who, by now, was spitting out her doughring. Annie caught Eileen's eye, who also began to laugh, but Kirsty had a wild look on her face.

"Get away. Get away," she yelled, and raising her arm, threw her doughring in his direction. It landed about six paces in front of him and bounced harmlessly against a gravestone.

Annie, shocked at the waste said, "What the Hell did you do that for?"

Eileen's head was right back, laughter gurgling in her throat. The old man, discomfited by the drama, half turned away.

"You silly bitch. I was wanting that doughring," said Annie.

At the sight of the retreating figure, and sobered by Annie's anger, Kirsty said, "Well bloody well buy your own."

Annie became aware of her cigarette and saw that distraction and the wind had virtually finished it.

"Shite," she said, and dropped it on the flattened soil. Eileen was still giggling and slapped Kirsty on the back.

19

"Wis it nae big enough for you, Kirsty. Would you rather he'd been better pleased wi' us?"

Kirsty angrily shrugged Eileen off.

"It was uninvited," she said.

She slid off the edge of the gravestone.

"I'm going back."

She was looking away from them.

'Well, I'm staying for my other fag. We won't get in yet, anyway. What about you, Eileen?" said Annie.

"Aye, well, since the entertainment took a turn for the better, I'll bide a bit." She winked at Annie.

Kirsty stood with her back to them, shoulders hunched. She took a step forward and stopped.

"Do you want a light?" called Annie.

She turned and came back. She kept her eyes to the ground and sat without a word. Lost in thought, long eyelashes trailing her cheeks, she seemed quite pretty.

Annie remembered the two matches and looked round for a corner. Bar walking back to the church doorway, there wasn't much shelter. Then she spotted what looked like a nook over by the cemetery wall.

"I'll go over there to light up."

She moved between the gravestones, crossed the path and edged her way to the wall. She pulled her arms half out of her blazer and hitched it up around her head. Cigarette in mouth, she crouched and struck a match. It caught and she pulled hard on it. She straightened up, wriggled back into the blazer, and, cigarette cupped in her palm, turned.

The dark-suited figure was standing in front of her, just off the path, his mouth squint in a silent snarl, fist thumping his groin. Even in the improved light it was impossible to discern bare flesh. But he was taking a chance. Annie glanced quickly up and down the path. Nobody was approaching. She could see the backs of Eileen and Kirsty beyond him. He'd decided against them and pursued her. Chosen her. He was making a sound in his throat. She looked into his eyes. If there had been even a spark of desperation she might have been afraid. His eyes were wrinkled and sad.

"Go on. Away you go," she said quietly.

He growled and thumped harder at himself. Her cigarette was burning down again.

"Away!" she said, louder and took a step towards him. He shuffled quickly backwards, threw her a last beseeching glance and turned, fumbling at his flies. She stood and watched him go.

LUNCH

"Christ! It's too bloody cold for that, mate," she thought, as she skirted the gravestones back to her pals. Eileen was turned, watching her. She couldn't be sure how much had been observed, or what had been made of it. She felt herself blush slightly.

"What do you think of that then?" she called.

Kirsty swung her head round.

"What?"

"The dirty wee bugger followed me."

"Who?"

"The Flasher," said Annie. "Your boyfriend."

Kirsty shot off the gravestone.

"I thought he'd gone. Come on. Let's go."

Eileen started sniggering, as she lit her cigarette off Annie's.

'He winna be back. Onywey, there's safety in numbers. If you get fed up we'll hae a gang-bang."

Annie and Eileen hooted at Kirsty's shocked expression till she began to relax.

"Well, if we're staying I'll have a drag," she said, reaching for Annie's cigarette.

"But you've got your own," said Annie.

Kirsty fixed her with a glare.

"I've only got one and it's for the bus."

Annie stared back. The best she could do was guess, and if she was wrong then Kirsty had won, whichever way you looked at it. She shrugged and smiled, stretching her cigarette in Kirsty's direction.

"Okay, if it'll steady your nerves after your ordeal."

Kirsty drew on the cigarette.

"Next time I come here it'll be with Dod."

Eileen sneered at her.

"Does your fiancé need to learn a trick or two, then?"

Kirsty lowered her eyes and with a smug smile said, "Oh no. My Dod knows it all."

Annie and Eileen winked at each other.

They heard, in the distance, the insistent ringing of the school bell.

"Christ!" said Eileen. "I'm on prefect duty. Quick!"

They threw their cigarettes in the dirt, pulled their blazers tight and sprinted for the back gate.

THE TEA-ROOM

Jane Struth

Feet clattered around the paved shopping centre. Shrill stilettos, metal-heeled bovver boots, leather brogues — they all goose-stepped in unison, their owners being oblivious to the sound of a regimental chorus. Colourful tubs of tulips and daffodils stood on guard, bowing stiffly to the army of feet.

So this is how the streets of Germany must have sounded, thought the woman, as she shrank amidst the tall tulips. Splintering of metal resounded in her ears causing an involuntary flinch. I must move quickly, she thought, as a strange feeling of panic began to grow. She marched blindly against the prevailing wave of people and looked straight ahead until her feet stopped abruptly outside a shop window.

Something grotesque caught her eye. Fascinated, she shuffled towards the offending display and as she drew nearer a great feeling of sadness welled within her. They have mutilated humanity, condemned us to this farcical puppet show: how could anyone be so cruel, thought the woman. It wasn't anger or injustice that caused her to shake, but total unashamed sadness.

Rows and rows of naked headless torsos hung limply from metal hooks, their necks decorated in paper ruffles. She sighed as the image of Mary Queen of Scots in her ruffled black dress swam before her eyes. A large juicy red apple seemed to be choking a pig with no body while several dismembered limbs lay amidst plastic parsley and tins of tomato soup.

Fat sausage-like fingers grasped a lamb's leg and stuffed it cheerfully into a brown paper bag. The fingers then handed the bag to a person who showed great dexterity at moving among hanging bodies. The person soon disappeared into the human flotsam.

An exhibition of Japanese prints looked promising. The image of the cool porcelain faces and finely decorated scrolls brought a calmness to the woman who stood motionless amidst the seething spectators. Already she felt more peaceful and casually admired her taller than usual reflection amidst the posters and paintings in the window.

Dark slanted eyes gazed out from a long oval face which was framed with a dark beret. I look oriental, she thought, secretly approving of the new image. Once inside the gallery she observed herself gliding gracefully among the exhibitions. Soon her lens hovered over a particularly attractive print.

Long leaves of foliage framed a mountain that could only be described as enchanted, as it stood in a lofty stance in an ethereal setting. Pastel pinks and mauves turned to a shimmering silver at the touch of a magical Goddess.

The woman mumbled something inaudible as she disappeared from the all-consuming eye of the camera. Once outside, the camera shifted its focus from the woman who was visibly wilting. I must sit down, she thought and quickly made her way towards a sign that said 'Tea-Room'.

Actually, she felt more in need of a stiff drink but did not quite know how to go about ordering one, even though the numerous bars looked quite friendly. However, the need to sit down determined the case and she soon found herself sitting in an old-fashioned tea room amidst clucking hens and ancient bunny girls.

One of the girls tottered towards her wearing a short black pelmet over ample buttocks. Once again, she was reminded of the butcher's shop but fought back the image of black pudding and ordered coffee and scones. The room buzzed as the black and white waitresses nodded like turkeys over their eager customers.

An enormous woman, who was seated across the aisle, caught her attention. She was carefully cutting a chocolate eclair into bite-sized portions. Yellow cream oozed from gashed slits onto her plump fingers. She licked each finger delicately then proceeded to pop the remaining bits down her throat. The picture was both fascinating and funny but the woman watching made a mental note to eat only one scone with a scraping of butter.

Hot breath played on her neck as the waitress left a display of objects on the table in front of her. She gazed somewhat fearfully at her purchase. It consisted of packets, little cartons, cutlery in plastic bags and a single scone wrapped in cellophane. Hopefully, she opened the coffee pot which contained two perforated bags floating in murky water.

Unhappily she swilled the contents of the coffee pot around and attacked the tiny container of cream. This task accomplished she sipped the liquid, which only had heat to its credit, and looked at the limp scone. Somehow it didn't seem worth the effort to unpick more bits of paper so she stuffed the scone into her pocket and sighed.

A man with a piece of sandwich stuck to his lip was glancing furtively between herself and a feathered green hat. The chocolate eclair woman looked rather uncomfortable squashed between table and seat. She wobbled all over and began to rise from the table. Cups and saucers shook as her thick leg pushed its way through some red table-cloth. Flashes of fat spilled over a doughy thigh and suddenly the apparition was standing, carefully collecting her small bits and pieces which consisted of handbag, hat and gloves. Calmly, and with light step, the enormous woman gracefully made her way through the crowded tea-room without as much as budging an elbow.

Sighing with relief and feeling very small and insipid, the woman paid for her coffee and left. Outside the clatter had ceased and she carefully made her way towards a bookshop. Something is wrong with the paving stones she thought with alarm: why are they so straight? The picture before her stretched into infinity like a perspective lesson while the tailor's dummy in a nearby shop took up the pose of a De Chirico painting.

A book outstretched its page and drew her in. She stood for a long time on the carpeted floor gazing in amazement at the typewritten words. What could they mean? She knew it was poetry because the cover said so, but it wasn't written in English nor did the words read across the page like a normal book. Vaguely, in the back of her mind she recollected something about sound poems. Indeed, she had once heard a poet read one of his creations at a poetry reading but he seemed to be having great difficulty reciting the words and she remembered thinking that he would lose his false teeth. Obviously this was one of those poems and with some relief she shut the book and stood back.

Kafka's large doleful eyes gazed from the corner of his *The Trial* but her fingers searched for a more reassuring author. Lawrence struck a sensible balance and, with certainty, she reached for a copy of *The Fox*. Her hand remained motionless and hung in mid-air as she remembered the glorious red brush of a fox's tail as it hung limply on the kitchen table. Abruptly, she brushed past the eager assistant who was guarding her till, and stumbled empty-handed into the seething street.

Beads of perspiration ran freely down her damp body. The sensation was not unpleasant, rather like that of a cool shower over a sunburnt body and for the first time the woman realized that she was unwell. The realization came as a shock but the necessity to reach safety and home was so overpowering that any attempt at thought was pushed aside.

Sunlight streamed through the mesh curtains glancing off the fragrant flowers which were arranged pleasantly beside her bed. The woman struggled out of her sandwich of covers, pushed back her hair and smiled.

SHARING

Wendy Stewart

Stephen stared out of the window at the bulk of the Maternity
block where lights were coming on in the wards. Twenty past, the
minute hand was just leaving the 4. He glanced down at his work;
the forms he was slowly completing, he picked up his pen, he felt like
bursting into tears.

"Think it's going to rain?"

On the other side of the room, Alison, his fellow clerk, paused in
her knitting.

"Looks like it." She put down her knitting and looked at her watch.
The clock on the wall was five minutes slow.

"The clock's wrong," he said, although they had known this since
the morning. Alison lit a cigarette and tossed the spent match into
the metal waste-basket.

"So you're going out tonight?" she said, smiling, "*another*
girlfriend? Anyone I'd know?"

"Hmn. No," he said, bent at his work.

"So you won't tell, huh? Where are you taking her?"

"Just a drink."

One of the telephones rang. Stephen grabbed it before it had time
to ring twice, thinking it might be *her*. It was George Bennet, their
boss.

"Steve, could you spare a few minutes? I want to go over the new
sickness benefit procedure."

"Okay, I'll be right over. Bennet," he replied to Alison's mute
inquiry. "I'll be a few minutes."

He left the office and crossed the reception area. There were no Out-patients on a Friday afternoon, but outside in the car park he saw the rear view of 'Claude' an old schizophrenic, slowly travelling towards the front gates.

"Claude!" he shouted, "Here!"

Claude turned at the sound of a familiar voice, escape forgotten, and slowly walked back.

"Claude," he said, "they want to see you upstairs."

"Who?" Claude asked, his mouth a plug of dried wrinkled skin, eyes unseeingly blank, his body frail and tense.

"José — up on the ward. They've been looking for you. Why don't you go up to the ward for a nice cup of tea. Eh?"

"What?" Claude asked.

"Up to the ward. For a cup of tea."

"Cuppa tea?"

"Yes, on the ward. On you go."

Claude shuffled off towards the stairs and Stephen continued towards the Administration building. Two years he'd been here. A minor cog. A few drips of rain spattered the tarmac in the car-park. Ahead and all around, lighted windows revealed the doll's house activities on the wards; people at work, tired-out workers accomplishing the business of dying. Middle-class doctors patching up the proles to get them fit to get back into the treadmill. In there was sickness and flowers, old men coughing, a steady flow of visitors, inhalations and exhalations, admissions and discharges.

He heard the clatter of dinner-trolleys being brought onto the wards, and also heard in the near distance an ambulance siren coming nearer. Probably RTA coming in to Casualty. He still felt the tears welling up. The sky was leaden grey, heavy. Any second now it would all fall around him. He didn't want to think about her. There should be a radio station broadcasting round-the-clock weeping as a form of therapy for the human race.

He reached the main corridor and walked past the dining room. He remembered meeting her in this corridor. He had seen her before briefly in the Main office. She was 20, had a short, neat hair style, a pretty, pert face with a dazzling eager beaver smile, large dark eyes; there was something kittenish about her. He had been unusually nonchalant, and had brought it off successfully. He usually felt grubby, grey, devoid of character, almost emasculated. He had taken her out for a drink at lunchtime on several occasions and this had developed into an evening outing when he had stayed all night with her. He had been surprised at the ease with which he had handled the situation. It had been a wonderful evening after which he could not have returned home even if she had wanted him to. After an evening like that to return to his flat would have been too depressing. He had never been more lonely in his life. He was Irish, and in some way an outsider also because of that. Loneliness affected him deeply. He mostly stayed in during the evenings because he could not bear to be seen out on his own. Evenings out were precious events.

They had walked into an ordinary pub and found it full of madness and jubilant anarchy; a jazzband played some sing-along standards, then a bunch of weird poets and impressionists, stand-up comics and men dressed in ballet tights, nazi helmets and evening jackets; bearded men with painted faces stood up and interrupted each other reading poems and singing rude ditties. Some poets read number poems made up only of numbers, others danced on the tables in heavy boots with carnations between their teeth.

They had walked away, dazed and dazzled, hand in hand and sat on her floor with coffees watching her portable TV, and when he kissed her, the first time, it had blossomed, despite the steady boyfriend 'she really liked'. John. He hated the name. He hated being first reserve — her bit on the side — and there was no sign that she'd ever chuck John in, as she had promised after that first night.

His eye was itching, he rubbed it, it began to water. He climbed the stairs to the main office, patting his hair, smoothing the edges, this cog, grinding along, common as muck. What kind of future? An older cog? A pensioned-off cog — moving slower in the same concentric circles? In an hour and a half the weekend would start. He'd see her for a few hours and then? Perhaps she'd tell him it was all off? As he passed the door of the main office he heard a burst of hilarity. He fancied he could distinguish her laugh from the others'.

He knocked on George Bennet's door

"Come in. Ah Stephen. Sit down. Be with you in a minute."

Bennet was scribbling furiously on a pad while he listened to the telephone cradled close to his ear by the pressure of his shoulder. Even he was a cog, albeit a bearded cog. Stephen had tried on several occasions to grow a beard but always gave up in embarrassment when it did not really grow in. He worked in the midst of girls and his appearance was constantly under criticism. He was the only male under 35 in the Psychiatric Unit.

"Right. Thanks for putting me in the picture. Fine. Bye."

Bennet replaced the receiver, turned to Stephen and reached for his pipe in the same movement.

"Notting Hill Carnival. We've got a special meeting on Medical cover."

He coughed politely. "Oh."

"Right, Steve. Here's the new procedure for sickness certification. Shouldn't affect your department that much, but I thought I'd better go over it with you . . ."

Stephen found his mind wandering into little clouds of nothingness, drifting off. He didn't know where his mind went when his concentration waned. Sometimes he knew the places it visited, but often it just drifted away and he wasn't thinking about anything; not a thing. Some place he'd never seen. One splash of rain hit the pane. One raindrop. And still the rain did not come. He remembered what she'd said on the phone and knew her boss had probably been in the room.

"Change of plan. I'll meet you after work. Would that be OK?"

"Yes," she said. "OK."

"The same place — front desk. Is that alright?"

"Right. Fine. Thank you," she said, as if he was merely a work colleague. But he'd slept with her. Was that all it was? It was as if she could give him all but could not give him everything. He didn't just want all of her some of the time, he wanted her every moment. His life was so complicated. Bennet finished speaking. He hadn't heard any of it.

"And when does this come into effect?" he asked.

"Well, as I just said, it's in effect now — or should be. The Department authorised 'self-certification' on the 17th July. Could you wait here for a moment. I'll be right back."

He left the room. Bennet was burly, and in his mid-thirties; a comfortable figure, well-settled, with a pretty wife in banking.

There was a round of laughter from the direction of the Main Office. He thought of her typing at her desk, v-neck blouse that showed everything if you stood behind her. She was so vulnerable — it made him sadder — almost sick — to think of other men looking at her, to think of her at other men's beck and call, all day, all week. He didn't want to be jealous, possessive — he had no right. It was a hopeless situation. And when lying in bed before dawn, she'd told him about losing her virginity at 14 on a bathroom floor he'd felt like getting up and leaving. And worse was to follow: At a party she'd let herself be taken by two boys at the same time. He felt ill thinking about it. In some ways it thrilled him. He remembered how she loved him to touch her, she had lain back and let him stroke her for hours. He had been afraid of hurting her at first, but there was no doubt that she enjoyed it. The thought had occurred to him that if she was double-crossing her boyfriend with him, she may also be double-crossing him with someone else. That was something he'd never be able to prove or disprove.

Bennet came back.

"Right Stephen, here you are — I got my Secretary to photocopy the new procedure. You know her don't you?"

Stephen stuck in the dream of her, her name, hesitated.

"Susan. My Secretary. You know. Big . . ." and Bennet cupped his hands at his chest.

"Oh yes," he said, "Susan. See you next week. Have a good weekend."

"Same to you."

He walked back to the Psychiatric Unit. Alison was chatting to Pat, one of the Medical Secretaries, when he returned. They hardly looked up as he came in. He pinned the procedure on the board and put his paperback and spectacles in his jacket pocket. Neither of the girls fancied him, though he could make both of them smile.

The rain cracked down suddenly onto the tarmac, onto the roofs of cars, cascading in knife-edged torrents. He ran to the vestibule and took out his cigarettes. He stood watching the water lancing down, enjoying his cigarette. There was a low mist which gave the high walls of windows an eerie look. The Dalton Wing: Department of Psychiatry. Two years he'd been here in this same job. The money wasn't good. There was the Union. He felt proud of the Union; he was a Shop-Steward and had taken a big part in the Health Services' Strike. He was notorious — one of half-a-dozen Union activists in the Hospital. He was one of thirteen summonsed by the Health Authority for illegally occupying the Administrator's office in protest at the Cuts. After nearly two weeks of occupation they had gone to the High Court and heard a judge describe them as 'highly committed and driven by the highest ideals'. Shortly after commanding them to vacate the Administrator's Office, this same judge had quashed the Health Authority's application for costs against them. That had been their finest hour.

People came in drenched, clothes sticking to their skin. He saw Annette, Susan's workmate going out. He didn't speak to her — they wanted to keep their liaison as secret as possible to avoid gossip.

At twenty past he climbed the stairs to the Main Office and timidly turned the handle — locked! She'd already gone!

He left the Hospital by the front gate, out into the rain, uncaringly oblivious of how wet he got and walked round to her bed-sit. He rang the bell. He felt betrayed and frightened. After a minute or two she answered, and opened the door.

"Is it alright?" he asked timidly.

"You must think I'm so stupid," she said, "I'm just stupid."

SHARING

"What do you mean?"

"Not meeting you. I honestly couldn't be bothered waiting. I just came straight home. I'm tired, I'm sorry."

"What do you want to do?"

"I don't know," she said, curling up in the corner of her bed.

"Eat?" he asked. "I'm starving."

"I fancy a Chinese."

"I know a really cheap one in Soho."

"I don't know if I could be bothered. There's a carry-out Chinese round the corner. The 'Hasty Tasty'. It's not bad. I want to watch 'Coronation Street' and 'Crossroads'."

"Oh God!" he said, laughing though he felt glum. Did he really fancy her? He studied her face; dazzling smile, large eyes with black pupils, her blue plastic ear-rings. She made a characteristic zestful shrug of her shoulders, snaking her lovely neck. He loved that movement. It was so playful, so 'little-girlish'. She was viviacious, zesty, alive.

"I want my mummy," he said laying his head on her lap. She laughed and ran her fingers in his hair.

"OK," he said, "you win, I'll go out for a carry-out. What do you want?"

"I've got a menu," she told him, smiling brightly.

After they had eaten their meal and drunk a little gin and tonic they sat on a large cushion at the side of the bed watching TV. Then, with his arms around her they kissed and cuddled. He removed her blouse and unclipped her bra and massaged her spine, kissing from the nape of her neck to her bottom, then they made love from the side, half-dressed, in front of the TV set with the sound turned down. Everytime he moved, her body jiggled, her breasts wobbled, which made him tremendously excited. She lay with her head arched right back as if her neck was broken. Her body was stretched out taut under him, every muscle straining tight.

Afterwards she stood up naked and pulled the curtains, turned out the light and they got into bed. He started to ramble deliriously. Daydreams from the edge of his mind. Living in cold water flats together in New York, Paris, Rome. Holding each other in foreign places. He talked and talked brilliantly; surrealist poetry of words, painting verbal pictures. He'd always been good with an audience of one.

"'Am I boring you?" he asked later.

"No. It's lovely. I like it. Keep talking. You're so nice. You look so nice."

Was it all an act? He wondered. She knew how to keep him happy.

31

How was it with John?

"What are you doing the rest of the weekend?" he asked.

"Tomorrow I'm meeting John. We're going to a party in the evening, and there's a barbecue in the afternoon."

"Nice. What are you doing on Sunday?"

"I've to meet friends — Paula and Jan. We're going to see a play."

He felt tangled up in jealousy, bitterness, depression, sick self-pity.

"What are *you* doing this weekend?"

"Me? Oh nothing planned. The pub probably." And inside he thought 'like hell'. He hated pubs — and never went on his own. It would be so miserable this weekend, boring and empty. If only she'd chuck John. He stapped another cigarette into his blotched face. He wanted to stop smoking. He hated cigarettes.

"I feel so bad," she said.

"About what?"

"About this. Being here with you. It'd be so much easier if you were a bastard." Bastard. He loved the flat sound; her Mancunian accent.

"What does Paula think about it?"

"She think's it's great. She thinks I should enjoy myself. She's a little bit angry — no — not angry — *jealous* at me having more than my fair share."

He was weak. A loser. A fall-guy. Every girl's hero but not the one they wanted to stay around for. He wasn't quite handsome. He could be witty. Underneath he knew he was a sexist pig. Couldn't help it. Tried to think of women as equal, tried to forget about marriage and possessiveness. But he wanted her forever. Still, he had his sensitivity. He was so sensitive he burst into tears when they said 'no'. 28. Twenty-eight years old. Unmarried. Unsettled. Depressed. Achieving what he wanted to — then finding out what he wanted was not what he had achieved.

The rain spattered uselessly on the street outside her open window, behind the curtains.

They drowsed in the night, their voices flying away into ever more wild fantasies. The rain beat steadily on the window sill. He imagined the street outside like the set for a 'film noir'.

"I snore," she told him, "*and* I talk to myself."

"I'll tape it and use it as evidence."

He kissed her below her ears. He could feel the sticky loose mass of her breasts against his chest as they pressed into each other and he kissed her lips. He felt tired. They lay for hours in uncomfortable positions until it looked as though they would never sleep.

SHARING

In the morning she got up early and bathed. Then she made tea and they finished off the prawn crackers, had a couple of cigarettes. The sun filtered though the curtains and there was the ever-hopeful prattle of early morning DJ's.

"I have to go soon," she said, "but you're welcome to stay."

"No — I'll go when you go."

Just then, a cat climbed in the window under the curtains. A beautiful black and white cat with a bell round its neck. It stood poised on the chair near the bed and watched them with interest. She picked it up and held it between her breasts.

"Watch — it'll scratch you," he warned.

"No it won't — will you kitty? Cats never scratch me. I've never been scratched in my life."

He got out of bed and dressed. It was a sunny morning. He kissed her and left.

AGAPE

Susan Campbell

I was staring out the smoky windows, watching the charred tenement faces slip by, their broken eyes and gaping door-mouths. The bus was for some reason intact, though the driver was half-dead, flopped over the wheel like a question mark. A large, round, yellow man cavorted along the outside, smirking behind his hand, pronouncing in thick black letters 'GLASGOW'S MILES BETTER'. Inside there was only me and my friend Chrissie up the front, and a lot of derelicts slumped in the back seats, missing their stop every time round and round in circles. So Chrissie my pal was going he said and SHE said, and wait till you hear, and patting me on the arm with her flippery hand, what with her sense of drama, when, from up my sleeve, rolling onto my raincoat lap, appeared the ring. It sat there, chucking light about, and my heart flopped over like a big caught fish. Then the ring was in my hand and in my pocket and Chrissie was still going she said he said and as the fish ceased its assault on my rib cage I looked up to find the burned-out eyes in the driving-mirror fixed on me.

So I had a think. Twenty minutes before, right, I was standing in a shop, gawping, with all these racks of fluffy jumpers and lead-lined suits, and the dried-up plants and bare girders, and the two lassies going haw haw etc. at the far end, when I saw that ring, sitting on its pedestal, with its glass dome on the floor beside it. I thought, better tell they lassies before some chancer takes a fancy to that. But then I thought, hang on. My Kev is up to his oxters in fornication, thinking I don't know. Cannae afford a ring to please her expensive Bearsden

34

taste and make it decent, and the minister thinking I cannae bring my
kid up right. Here's ma chance. I'll do a wee wrong thing and prevent
a greater evil.

But then I thought, no, two wrongs make double trouble, as my
Mam used to say.

But then I thought, seeing as I'm one of the Underprivileged, my
husband terminally unemployed, people spraying Nuke The Pope
on my lobby etcetera, why should I not get a wee free gift for a
change, seeing as it's not for me.

But then I thought, stealing's a sin however you look at it, and I'll
burn in Hell, and all of a bustle I turned and nearly ran out and up to
the bus-stop before I could change my mind, my skin hot and
crawling, and there I met Chrissie with her hesaid shesaid and here I
find the thing had got itself stuck up my sleeve somehow.

So there was a different game, and I sat there on the bus, mulling it
over. Was it stealing if something fell into my lap? Or was the ring
meant to save Kevin from the big fire? The bus stopped at a traffic
light and a wee boy shouted EVEnin' TIAMS from the pavement. He
was sitting, legless, on a trolley and his newsboard said OUTRAGE
in huge print, and I thought this ring could be a tiny link in God's
plan. A man in an overcoat came up and shoved the boy round the
corner and started hawking an inflatable dome with free mask. The
bus moved off, not that the lights had changed, since they'd all been
broken for days, and I thought to myself, mibbe I passed a wee test
back there, seeing I didn't take it, and this is my reward. I was getting
fond of that one too, till we reached our stop, and as we got off that
old driver opened one ashy eye to give me a wink, and I felt my guilt
kindle, and knew then that my thought was sinful. We crossed the
wasteland, stepping over the rubble where the tenements had been,
and the guys lying there in heaps, stinking to heaven, and by the
time I'd said goodnight to Chrissie and watched her hirple off, and
climbed the stairs, skirting the sodden bundles slumped about the
landings, I'd made up my mind to take it back.

Kevin was out, and Peter, my husband, was sitting in his chair
saying nothing as usual, so I put the TV on and made him his tea, and
by the time I sat down it was the News and Shock Horror the enemy
was approaching and thousands were dead in the streets and that,
just like every night, and my mind wouldn't stay on what I was
watching but kept on wandering back to the ring in my raincoat
pocket in the cupboard. So finally, even though it was getting dark, I
thought I'd take my life in my hands and walk along to the church for
some of that spiritual sustenance to keep me right. Off I goes,
buttoned into my raincoat, making Peter a cup of tea first, and one of

the biscuits to keep him quiet, and as I was crossing the wasteland, I saw this shell of a car, black and buckled with fire, the top gaping, the wheel sockets empty. Far from the streetlights and it was all dusk and drizzle and dodgy underfoot with the stray animals but something or other made me swerve from the way I was going and make towards the car, and as I got closer I saw inside the shadows locked and heaving. I went right up to it, looked in the broken top, and there was Kevin and his trollop making the beast with two backs over the bare springs of the front seats. She was going him like a racing bike and my wee boy staring up at the sky with a dead look in his eye, and his mother with her face tripping her. I made not a sound but backed off to walk quietly home again. Oh but my insides had hardened and I knew then what the something or other was that led me to the car on my way to the church to show me what to do. To save them from this unholy coupling, like dogs in the debris, I was to give him the ring in the morning.

But by the time I'd got Peter up and sat him in his chair and organised him, Kevin had slunk off to the site, crook-eyed, close-mouthed, never giving me the chance to have a word. It would keep till teatime, or so I thought. But when I'd done the dishes and went to tidy the shelter under the stairs, there on the floor was the Good Book, lying open. Peter, for reasons best known to himself, had been reading it there in the night, the deep one. I picked it up and looked at the face it presented. The Sermon On The Mount. I dropped it and a dead black bird fluttered to the spiralled carpet. Thou Shalt Not Steal! Heed the Word, thought I, especially when it's squawked in your ear, and I went to get my coat with its little-lumpy pocket. On my way out I patted Peter goodbye and he crumbled into a heap of ashes. Not touched for too long.

Toiled across the wasteland, clutching my pocket to keep faith, the dirty yellow metal sky a great dome, like inside an eggshell, with all around the broken horizon. As I laboured forward towards the city the dust and filth was rising in a cloud and the yellow sky went black and the weak old sun was blotted out, and as I crossed the road to the shop, I was hit by a bloody great bus. As I performed a graceless somersault, I beheld in my dead shadow, spreading on the concrete, a bug-eyed beastie, fallen broken-winged, clinging to the tilt of the turning world, eyes and mouth open to the heavens, expectant, agape. Fast and huge below me it ballooned. I landed, it splattered, and here I find myself, my crushed limbs arranged, being goggled at by masked faces. Salt water mingles with blood in my mouth, wide with praise and wonder that I live. The masked faces float by, sea-monsters in the thick air, and now the sirens begin to wail.

AFTERNOON NAP

Joy Pitman

She'd get a sleep this afternoon.

Definitely.

Nothing, no nothing was going to stop her.

Ellie heaved the pram up the step, feeling the extra weight of the shopping pull the muscles tight across her back. But even in her icy-clear, seven-foot tall state of consciousness — which she had learnt to recognise as a product of total weariness — the effort gave her a sense of satisfaction. Another small triumph against time and the multitude of trivial tasks which reproduced themselves and raced ahead of her in an infinite line, however hard she tried to keep pace and demolish them. She had saved herself some extra seconds by making only one trip to the front door, instead of going first with the shopping and then a second time with Ian — now grizzling for his feed — and the wretched, cumbersome pram.

By now the machine would have switched off washing and she could perhaps start the nappies rinsing while she fed the baby.

Maybe she could even bear to listen to the inevitable rising crescendo of cries while she put the shopping away. Surely he could wait just ten minutes more.

If only everything could be done. If only there could miraculously be no uncompleted chores before the next round of feed-and-change-and-prepare-and-cook-and-clear came round again. Then she could sleep for as long as Ian slept.

To hell with the dust in the hall and Joe's upturned nose and frown of disapproval, "Such a pity you don't like housework." To hell with whether tea was on time, "Why do you complain that I'm late home if the meal's never ready?"

To hell with it all, just for today.

She manoeuvred the pram through the doorway into the kitchen and sat on a chair, stealing the precious few seconds she had just won and absently rubbing the small of her back with her knuckles.

She would die if she didn't get some sleep soon. These last ten weeks she'd begun to understand those tales of torture by sleep deprivation. If it went on like this, she'd be stretched so thin she'd become transparent and simply vanish.

"Don't think about it now," she told herself, "you'll just start to cry": already feeling her chest expand with a painful breath and her stomach shrink to a tight knot, the dryness in her throat.

She imagined the beautiful, soft, waiting bed, and snuggling down to sleep with Teggy. Teggy had been her faithful, comforting companion ever since she was two. His fur was terribly worn, and his paws virtually threadbare, but his glass eyes were still as bright and friendly, his shape as huggable and yielding.

"Just get through the next hour, then you can sleep."

When would she ever get more than two or three hours at a stretch? When do babies usually start to spend the whole night asleep like civilised beings? Helen up the road seemed to have managed. She told Ellie how her second, Jennifer, had slept from eleven to six at only five weeks.

Mechanically she set about putting the butter and cheese in the fridge.

All those well-thumbed baby books didn't really help either. 'The rate of development varies vastly from child to child.'

She stacked the tins on the shelf and put the onions and mushrooms on the side, ready to do something with tonight.

Ian's grizzle was now turning into a definite cry.

"Hang on, hang on," she found herself saying. "Just let me get these nappies going."

She bent over the steaming washer, lifting the heavy wet bundles into the spinner. When they'd decided against the cost of an automatic, two years ago, she hadn't known about the daily piles of stinking nappies, pee-soaked babygros and sicked-on shirts of her own that a tiny baby creates.

Why had no-one told her?

There was a monstrous conspiracy of silence about it all.

An air of assured competence surrounded the other young mothers she encountered at the Child Welfare Clinic on Tuesday afternoons. Perhaps, she wondered anxiously, she was the only one who found it so hard. The one time she had tried to talk to the Health Visitor about her doubts she had been met by a cheerful incomprehension and phrases like 'just needs a firm routine'.

Come to think of it, it was the same Miss Fleming who had impressed upon them at the ante-natal classes the importance of getting in an afternoon nap. "You young mums need to keep your strength up: you'll have a baby to look after, as well as a husband."

Who looks after mothers, Ellie had absently wondered.

The other week she had confided in Helen how tired she'd been feeling, hoping for some sympathy, or at least, recognition from a fellow victim. Helen had responded with a bustling evasion, and talked about 'duty to one's family'. Helen was a regular church-goer, and Ellie secretly thought she looked positively abounding in long-suffering and Christian endurance.

Her breasts began to tingle as Ian's cries rose louder and more insistent. That tug tugging of sound at her belly, her uterus, as though there was a second umbilical cord, invisible but strong and elastic, stretching between her and this demanding little creature, no matter how great the physical distance which separated them. A cord the midwife couldn't cut.

She thrust the hose onto the tap, adjusted the flow and shut the lid.

Now for Ian.

As she lifted him out of the pram, the tingling in her breasts grew into an ache, but one she found oddly pleasant, an anticipation of relief to come. Shifting the baby round to lie in the crook of her arm, she felt a familiar warm sogginess communicate itself through her sleeve. In the maternity hospital they'd taught the mums to change baby before *and* after feeds. But she'd soon realised the implications of that one when she had to do all the washing herself. In any case, feeding appeared to set off a chain reaction, and he always seemed to dirty the nappy immediately afterwards. Like a fleshy little conveyor belt where she poured herself in at one end and wiped up the excrement at the other.

Ellie undid her shirt with one hand and unhooked her maternity bra.

The cries ceased.

She felt the pull at her left nipple and settled back against the kitchen chair. Enforced stillness for ten minutes, twice over. She relaxed into the pleasure of giving. Feeding gave her a positive sensuous delight. The first time she had felt it, it came as a shock of surprised joy she hadn't expected to discover. She stroked the soft down on the rounded little head. He looked so lovely; so lovable and contented at these moments.

She reached for the Magaret Drabble she'd left on the table at the ten o'clock feed, but the print danced and swayed in front of her eyes.

"God, but I'm tired," she sighed aloud.

She thought aloud a lot nowadays, held numerous one-way conversations with her captive and diminutive audience.

When Ian's time was up on the first side, she put him over her shoulder to wind and walked across to turn off the machine.

She sat down again and rearranged her bra. While Ian sucked and dozed at her right breast, Ellie mentally prepared the tea.

A casserole wouldn't do. She'd have to get it ready now in order to leave it long enough to simmer, and then she'd lose some of that sleep she'd promised herself. It would have to be something simple. There was still some bacon. Yes. Spaghetti with bacon, mushrooms, onions and herbs. It could all be ready quickly and the spaghetti go on whenever Joe came through the door.

Since entering the state of motherhood, her life had turned into a time-and-motion puzzle, to be solved by female cunning and foresight.

Upstairs now for the nappy.

At least she'd finally learnt to fold the clean one before she started. She'd suffered several despairing early attempts when this omission had left an unfortunate thirty second gap between smearing the zinc and castor oil on the tiny red bottom and wrapping the nappy round. In this brief moment Ian had invariably peed in a beautiful arc over his knees, leaving a puddle on the changing mat which had flowed straight up into his vest, so she'd had to dress him all over again.

She had the changing routine licked now, she thought smugly, snapping the safety-pin shut.

She put the contented and now docile child into his cot, kissing him gently on his warm, smooth cheek.

Sleep.

Damn! The washing. She'd have to hang it up now or it would still be there when she wanted to start cooking.

Wearily she stumbled downstairs again and prised the nappies from the wall of the spinner, throwing them into the basket.

She was racing time. If she won, she could sleep.

Oh, for that blessed quiet and nothingness and calm.

She glanced at the hands of the kitchen clock as she moved automatically back and forth. Ten to three. Ian had only had ten minutes so far, she reassured herself. There was lots of time left until he woke.

AFTERNOON NAP

She'd forgotten to feed herself yet again, but took a chocolate digestive and an apple and placed them at the foot of the stairs while she paused to take the phone off the hook. Yesterday's attempt at a lie-down had been foiled by a foolish decision to cook chicken and a phone call from Helen who wanted a last-minute baby-sitter. Ellie couldn't promise her in any case, as Joe often went back to work on the computer after tea. Frank might seem a bit dull, but at least school exercise books and Latin dictionaries were portable, and Helen could rely on him being home most evenings.

She gulped down the biscuit and climbed the stairs.

At last, at last, into the bedroom, to bed.

She picked up Teggy from the chest of drawers and set him on the pillow with a smile, crunching greedily on the apple. As she took off her shoes and jeans she recalled how incredulously Joe had greeted Teggy's removal to their marital home after the wedding. "Damn it all, Ellie love, you're not a child any more." But when he saw her stunned and uncomprehending face, he'd relented, "As long as I don't have to share my *bed* with the bloody thing."

Ellie slid her aching body under the downie and drew Teggy to her. He nestled so snugly under her chin. She sniffed the reassuring, undefinable scent of him.

Her eyes closed.

She was drifting.

Oh. No, not now. It couldn't be.

It was. A faint but perfectly distinct little wail from Ian's room. She put Joe's pillow over her free ear and prayed he'd stop soon.

But she could still hear.

Nothing could cut her senses off from her child. Even when asleep, she woke if he merely whimpered. Why didn't Joe? It wasn't worth prodding him awake and arguing him into doing something if Ian woke between feeds. After all, as Joe pointed out, *he* needed his sleep; *he* had a job of work to do. Even in the hospital Ellie had slept through the cries of the other women's babies, but never through those of her own. 'Imprinting', her brain spelt out with irritating clarity. Or was that only baby monkeys and goslings, she asked her brain back in confusion. And what the hell difference did it make, anyway?

It was no use: the cries were getting louder.

With resignation she swung her feet over the edge of the bed and padded through into Ian's room.

Wind? A dirty nappy?

She tested her hypotheses. It was too soon for teething yet, surely. But he'd stopped already, and was sleeping against her shoulder.

41

Gently, holding her breath in trepidation, Ellie laid him in the cot, pulling the covers over as carefully as she could.

She tiptoed back into her haven.

Ah, that lovely drifting between waking and sleeping, when the spinning of her mind round the minutiae of the day slowed and ceased. She was falling softly backwards, sinking into a cocoon of darkness.

Jerk!

Her limbs insistently convulsed her awake as a thin drawn-out wail sent its accurate lance straight into her guts.

She leapt from the bed and burst into Ian's room, grabbed him roughly, set him howling even more furiously at this frightening and unknown figure, and ran blindly downstairs with him into the kitchen.

"There!" she cried, her voice harsh with suppressed despair and rage. "Howl yourself to death in here then!"

She thrust him into the pram and found herself propelled by some unseen, powerful momentum through the kitchen door, slamming it noisily behind her, and pounding up the stairs, great sobs tearing their way through her teeth.

She flung herself on the bed and felt an inert form beneath her arm. She picked him up in a fierce and desperate grasp, the tears blurring his well-known features.

"Shut up! Shut up! Shut up!" she shouted, pounding his little body rhythmically on the pillow. "I want to sleep, I want to sleep, I just want to sleep. Shut up! Shut up!"

Then, in a crazed and dreamy horror, Ellie watched while his precious round head removed itself neatly from his body and rolled onto the floor.

The scream gathered itself in her belly and rose in slow motion through her chest to issue, detached, enormous and remote, from her open mouth.

* * *

She was floating on a bright, white sea of silence; her tears exhausted; empty.

The quiet ticking of the bedside clock gradually penetrated her consciousness.

It hardly seemed to matter any more whether she slept or not, so that when the door-bell rang, Ellie automatically got out of bed and looked down from the window to see who was calling.

She recognised the grey, permed hair and blue uniform of the Health Visitor. Taking her dressing-gown from the hook and pulling it hastily round her, she made her way downstairs to open the door.

Miss Fleming gave her usual enthusiastic smile, then took in Ellie's unkempt look, bare feet, and dressing-gown.

"Just up from your nap, dear?"

Ellie felt her head moving in imitation of a nod.

"Oh good. That's very good. It's so important to keep fit in these early days," she leant forward and touched Ellie confidentially on the arm, "especially when you're feeding."

Then, to the real business of the visit, "And how's baby today?"

"Sleeping," Ellie managed to croak. He was silent, anyway.

"In that case, we won't waken him," beamed Miss Fleming. "You've been keeping up with your appointments at the Clinic now, haven't you?" She rifled in her brief-case and drew out a little blue card. "Yes. Nearly time for his three month check up. But I'm sure you've nothing to worry about on that score. Such a beautiful little fellow you've got there, Mrs Maurice." She sighed.

Ellie stared at her, too stunned by the woman's obvious delight in her private vision to utter any word which might disturb it.

"Well, we'll expect to see you on Tuesday, then."

Miss Fleming started edging down the steps, but turned to give Ellie a final smile, "Glad to see you're getting your rest, my dear."

OUR COUSIN CHRISSIE

Elizabeth Case

Auntie Net's annual visit always caused an argument between our father and mother.

"Who does she think she is anyway, coming up here like Lady Muck?"

"I'll not have you say another word against my sister. She's been very good to all of us."

"Aye, handing down her old clothes. I canny say I like to see my wife and weans in other folks' cast-offs. And sending us food as if we wis starving."

It was 1934 and the Shipyard had been closed for two years now. Mother always made sure though that, even if he was out of work, Father had a shilling in his pocket. She had heard about a man found in the waters of the harbour with nothing in his pocket, and they called him destitute.

"Well, it's nice to be able to put a decent Sunday dinner on the table for once."

Mother lifted the hot ashet carefully from the kitchen range. On it sat a roast chicken in golden-brown perfection, the smell of it quite literally making our mouths water. It wasn't often we had a dinner like this nowadays. Mostly it was soup and bread with a bit of bacon or sausage if we were lucky.

"That's right, cast up to me that a man on the dole can't feed his family."

But my father forgot to sound bitter because he was looking at the succulence on the plate before him.

"Ah well, who's for a bit of chookie birdie then?" he said brandishing the carving knife.

My wee sister, Jean, stared at him in horrified disbelief.

"'Sno' a birdie, Daddy, is it?"

"No, no, pet. Your Daddy's only funning. Come on now and eat your dinner."

When we had all wiped the last speck of gravy from our plates Father returned to the fray.

"When are they coming to visit their needy relatives then?"

"They're coming this afternoon," Mother said placidly, gathering up the dishes. "They'll be here for their tea."

Oh well, I thought, that'll be ham for the tea then. I knew there was some in the big box that arrived yesterday, and anticipation of another good feed made bearable the prospect of an afternoon spent with that wee scunner, Chrissie.

Auntie Net had gone off to England when she was young and taken a job as a housekeeper to a widower. Although he was a good bit older it wasn't long till she married him and Chrissie was born. He was dead now, and she was left very well off. Chrissie was a year older than me and so they thought her clothes would fit me, but they didn't. She was a different shape from me, and anyway I felt daft wearing such fancy things.

They arrived that afternoon from the best hotel where they were staying for the week. Our room and kitchen wouldn't be good enough for them with their airs and graces and their English voices — yes, Auntie Net, too. Chrissie's hair curled bright and shiny where mine was lank and straight. Her figure was curved even more than last year. She probably ate chicken every day of her life.

Auntie Net kissed everybody, including Father, who leapt back as if she had stung him. My brother, Danny, tried to escape by dodging behind me, but she caught him, too. Chrissie just smiled and said "Hello," as if she was really glad to see us. But she was too high and mighty to kiss us just the same.

I had a good idea that Auntie Net sent Mother money though Father chose to ignore it. He hated charity, as we all did, but five of us couldn't live on the little that was coming into the house. I would have to leave school next month when I was fourteen and try to find a job though my teachers wanted me to stay on, and Danny had another year to go.

"Flora, why don't you and the others take Chrissie out for a nice walk?"

Mother would be wishing she could send Father out, too, so as she and Auntie Net could have a good crack, but he was sitting there in his chair like the beggar at the feast.

At least it was something to do.

"Come on," I said, "you'll not need coats."

Chrissie was wearing a pink suit with a pleated skirt and a pillbox hat to match. White gloves completed the outfit. I couldn't wait to see the street's reaction to that.

We went out the door and down the stairs. I noticed Chrissie wrinkling her nose as we passed the lavvy on the landing and wondered what she would do if she had to "go" before she got back to the hotel. The smell of the close was so familiar to me that I never noticed, but now I tried to analyse what was in it. The mustiness of the walls, the bleach the women used to clean the steps, the cloying smell from the lavatories, and now as we approached the bottom, the stink from the Kerrigans' house, cabbage, dirty nappies, sour milk, unwashed human flesh.

As we passed their door the Kerrigan twins popped out as usual.

"Where're yez gaun? Kin we come?"

Chrissie's face reflected her disbelief, dismay and compassion. The twins were filthy, their clothes mere rags and the thin legs stuck into broken boots were bare of socks.

"Right, come on," I said.

Outside we met Matt Wilkie from the next close, and my heart gave a flutter. He was sixteen and apprenticed to a plumber. He was good-looking, too, and I had just decided to fall in love with him. Danny worshipped him because he played football well. He looked us over casually, then his eyes swivelled back to Chrissie.

"Hullo there," he said.

He was saying it to us all, but his eyes were still on Chrissie. After a moment she gave him one of those smiles of hers, all white teeth and shining eyes.

"Hello," she said. "I'm Chrissie."

"And I'm Matt. Where are you going?"

"Oh, just for a walk," I said discouragingly.

"Mind if I come, too?"

I wouldn't have minded at all if it had been just us, but if he was going to be hanging around Chrissie, well . . . Still there was nothing I could do about it. And before we set off we had another addition to the party. The Dummy came up at his usual shambling run and tagged on.

Nowhere in our town is far from the sea. To the right was the esplanade where the holiday-makers enjoyed themselves. There wouldn't be so many of them these days paddling at the edge of the sea with their trousers rolled up, rowing themselves in wee boats,

46

eating penny cones. The big houses on South Beach would be let by the month, fathers on the golf course, families on the sands, but with all the unemployment on Clydeside there wouldn't be many of our kind of holiday-maker. Those were the ones who were willing to sleep six to a bed. We let them the front room and use of the kitchen for a fortnight. They did say Mrs McNaught from round the corner was still meeting the trains from Glasgow, but she couldn't be having much luck.

Instead of making for the esplanade I turned left in the direction of the harbour. It was a walk we often took, through the empty shipyard where the grass was growing, over the swing bridge to the breaking-up yard. Sometimes you could get on to the stripped hulls of the old ships though you had to be careful.

Matt and Chrissie were chatting away, playing pat-a-ball with words. They were too busy measuring each other up to notice where they were going. The others were used to following my lead. We picked our way over the deserted railway lines, through the big gates that swung uselessly on their hinges and along the side of the dry dock. A rabbit scampered away at our approach. Some of the men trapped them to make a meal for their families.

We came to the swing bridge that spanned the gap at the entrance to the inner basin. Danny ran over it first, then one of the Kerrigan twins, sending it rocking and swaying a little. Chrissie hesitated. Matt swaggered over to show her how easy it was and paused near the other end. I got up on to it at our end and motioned to Chrissie to pass me, showing her how to hang on to the side-ropes. She started out gingerly, then gained confidence. Her little, white-sandalled feet sounded hollowly on the boards.

As she reached the middle I raised my hand in a signal. Danny and one Kerrigan at their end and I and the other twin started to push the ends of the bridge from side to side. The Dummy jumped on behind me and helped, laughing soundlessly. Chrissie in the middle found herself swaying alarmingly in a sickening motion. It was a thing we often did to one another, but Chrissie was made of gentler stuff than us. I couldn't see her face but I could hear her scream. It satisfied some savage need in me.

Matt yelled, "Stop that! Stop it for Chrissake!"

He couldn't make up his mind what to do, whether to turn and stop the two behind him or whether to go back and rescue Chrissie. But he could scarcely move either.

Suddenly there was a horrible, splintering sound. The old wood of the bridge had snapped. Chrissie's legs went through the gap, and for one long second she hung there, clutching desperately at the

47

ropes. Then she slowly slithered into the muddy water.

It was Matt who jumped in and got her out. It was Matt who carried her, muddy and bleeding, along the road home while the·rest of us followed in miserable procession. The Dummy ran backwards and forwards, like a sheepdog, uttering his uncouth sounds.

Much, much later, after all the hysteria and the recriminations and the other excitements were over, we were shut in the room in disgrace. At least Father hadn't taken his belt to us, but he might still do it. I brought out the tumbler I kept for the purpose and put it against the wall to hear what they were talking about in the kitchen.

Mother was saying, ". . . never be back here again, that's for sure."

Well, that should please him, I thought. But when Father spoke it was in a bleak, flat voice as if all the spirit had gone out of him.

"Will she stop sending the money, d'ye think?"

"Our Net's no' like that." Mother was trying to comfort him. "She's not one to hold a grudge, and the girl did say it wasn't the weans' fault. But even — even if she did we'd manage somehow."

"How, Annie? How?"

I had never seen my parents embrace, but somehow I could picture them now with their arms round each other, holding on.

I lay down on the bed and covered my head with the blankets to hide the tears that streamed down my face. They were not tears of remorse or even of self-pity. They were tears of anger at the society that made pride a luxury my father couldn't afford.

DIARY OF A SOCIALITE

Joyce Begg

January 1st.

Now that a new year has begun, I am about to put my first resolution into practice, that is to keep a proper diary, not the kind I used to keep when I was a child, with entries such as 'Today it rained. Practised piano for forty minutes. Had chicken pie.' This is going to be the real thing, the kind of literary tour de force that people will unearth in a couple of hundred years, and publish as a marvellous record of the time, full of detail, humour, and insight. The only fly in the ointment is that I shan't be around to collect the royalties. However, it's only money, and of that I have enough, thanks to Mother's far-sightedness.

My mother is a remarkable woman. I don't like her much but she has got her priorities absolutely right. She knew exactly what she was doing when she married Father, and she knew exactly what she was doing when she married B.H. I know little of my father except what Mother told D. and me, but by all accounts he was a nice old man with plenty of money and a fondness for the bottle. I don't know whether he was an alcoholic before their marriage or as a result of it, but it doesn't matter either way. When he died he left enough for all of us. D. and I have never had to work. I had a bash at secretarial college, but it didn't appeal, and D.'s finishing school threw her out. B.H. left us hardly anything but his name and an entrée into the higher echelons. Much good it has done us so far. However, this being January 1st, we live in hope.

It is snowing like billy-o out of this window.
I think it's supposed to be a lamb chop casserole for dinner. I hope
there's a decent pudding.

January 2nd.

If this is to be a true record of events, there is no point in
pretending that I am not in a foul mood today. I wasn't when I got
up, but D. is enough to reduce a saint to thoughts of murder, or at
least grievous bodily harm. I think D. is simple. She is fat and silly.
Why anyone her age — thirty-two — should want to play in the snow
at all I cannot imagine. It irritates me just to think about it. But what
really gets on my wick is the way she borrows things without
thinking, and ruins them in the process. She has perfectly good boots
of her own, but whose does she put on to play in the snow? Mine. My
new suede knee-high boots. She has got white wavy lines on the
leather, and has probably burst the zip fasteners. She has fat feet,
while mine are long and slender. I really do think she is simple. She
doesn't even have that winning grace that simple people often have.
She is plain and stupid.
Spareribs. Sometimes I think C. is a rotten cook.

January 3rd.

Isn't it amazing how things can be stood on their heads? There I
was yesterday getting all steamed up about D., and then today the
whole world looks a different place. Even the snow seems to be
melting a bit. And now for the news. We have received an *invitation*.
At long last B.H. is doing us a bit of good. We have been invited out
before, of course, but mainly to boring dinner parties where the
women are snooty and the men all over sixty. Where's the romance
in that? We've never been to St. Moritz or Henley or anything. This,
however, is something completely different. This may well be my *big
chance*. And D.'s too, if she plays her cards right, but that's not quite
so likely. P.C. has finally got around to including us on his social list,
and one can only wonder that it's taken him so long. I thought we
might make it to the party on the river last June, but we didn't,
although Mother worked herself into a decline on our behalf. I'll say
that for her, she's a trier.
I'll need a new dress. Deep red would suit me, with my dark hair
and my eyes, but I'm not sure about the style. The empire line is

DIARY OF A SOCIALITE

supposed to flatter the small busted figure. As soon as the snow is drivable, we'll go out to look for material. D. fancies pink. I told her she'd look like candy floss, but she's determined. More fool her. No one's going to look at her anyway, but if she wears pink they will positively turn away.

Chicken à la king tonight. Very suitable.

January 8th.

I've been so very busy that I'm afraid I have neglected my diary. So much for resolutions. However, now that the material is bought and the fittings have commenced, there is a brief lull in which to take stock. This is when I should come up with these pieces of insight, — such as 'Everything comes to her who waits' — with which to astound posterity. For it is true. We have done all the right things, been seen in all the right places, entertained the right people, and at last it is paying off. This ball is going to be the event of the year, bar none.

A funny thing happened at lunch today. C. brought in the soup as usual — cock o' leekie (not bad) — and lingered behind to talk about the dresses. D. and I described our respective outfits — D. did go for the pink and it's going to be truly awful — and C. said something that reduced us all to silence, followed by hysterics. She asked what she was going to wear. Honestly, you could have knocked me down with an aerosol. The poor soul thinks she's coming with us. I thought D. was simple, but C. has her beat hands down. She went on about being B.H.'s daughter and just as entitled — oh, it was pathetic. It was actually embarrassing. She seems to have no proper pride whatsoever. I mean, she'd be right out of place at a function like that. And she'd *feel* it. It would be like trying to graduate from university with two 'O' Levels.

The snow has gone, but a hard frost has set in.

January 14th.

Tomorrow is the Big Day, and I cannot think of anything else. My dress is gorgeous. Although people are becoming more casual these days, there are occasions when nothing but the classically grand will do, and this is one of them. We have every confidence of a successful outcome.

51

January 16th.

In the tradition of the late great Samuel Pepys, I should be able to give an accurate account of who all was there, what they wore, what they said, and infuse the whole thing with my own witty observation. Frankly, I'm cheesed off. There was not one man there worth wasting time on, except P.C. himself, and he was fully occupied. What is the point of getting all dressed up, and dragging out the family tiaras, if one is going to spend the time leaning against a pillar, or dancing with a chinless youth who comes up to your collar bone? Although she won't admit it, D. was pretty short of partners too. Mind you, she looked terrible. Not really candy floss, more of a pink zeppelin. She said I looked like a traffic light. It's amazing how jaundiced D. can sometimes sound.

The food was good, which was something. Smoked salmon, quails in aspic, the usual sort of thing, but well presented.

A funny thing happened half way through the evening. This strange girl appeared that no one seemed to know, although I'm sure I've seen her somewhere before. Perhaps at Ascot. Anyway, whoever she was, P.C. took a terrific shine to her, danced with her all night, took her out on to the terrace. Actually, although one hates to say it of one's host, it was kind of ill-mannered.

She left early, which was something. The only thing is, it didn't seem to bring P.C. back into the general melée. He kept wandering around with this shoe in his hand, an unusual shoe, I grant you, but a shoe just the same. I mean, who walks around at a function like that carrying a shoe? It was made of high grade perspex from the look of it. Like crystal, only bendy. Very odd.

It is raining.

I think P.C. is boring.

January 17th.

Something has happened to the kitchen. No one has painted it or anything; in fact it is most difficult to describe. It's glittery. Everything in the kitchen is glittering. I don't understand it. Another thing I don't understand, especially with the kitchen looking so bright, is why C. is looking so terrible. I don't know what's wrong with her, but she keeps crying. Her eyes are red and incredibly ugly. I can't imagine what she's got to cry about. *Her* hopes haven't been dashed. No one has ignored *her* social aspirations. She hasn't got any. Maybe it's the mice. We appear to have a small plague of them. Mother told C. to set traps but she said she'd rather not.

The soup was too salty. Sausages for main course. Definitely substandard. I complained to C. I don't think she heard me.

January 18th.

No one in two hundred years' time is going to believe a word of this. I don't believe it myself. P.C. is still wandering about carrying the shoe. He is now working his way through the guest list till he finds the owner. Apparently every female who was at the ball has to try on the shoe. One or two people have tried to pull a fast one, but no one has managed to convince him yet.

A strange car has just drawn up. It is a Rolls with a flag on the . . .

It didn't fit. It didn't bloody fit. But at least it didn't fit D. either.

P.C. is a twit.

January 19th.

Enough of these strange goings on. It is time to offer more serious reflections for posterity.

It's raining again.

Nothing has happened since yesterday.

There's that car back again.

January 24th.

I don't know how to put this. The whole thing is so incredible that I don't know how to frame it so that it constitutes a faithful record. I don't know if I want a faithful record. It has taken me several days to absorb what happened.

I may as well tell it from the beginning. P.C.'s car returned, and this pompous major domo type got out and remonstrated with Mother on the doorstep, insisting that according to the electoral roll there was another female in this house of voting age. Mother said that was perfectly true, but on his previous visit P.C. had only mentioned the guest list, not the electoral roll. However, Mother was only too pleased to see P.C. again and invited him and the major domo/chauffeur in for a drink. They refused any refreshment, P.C. saying he was anxious to complete his search. Mother sent for C., and up she came from the kitchen, complete with rubber gloves gloves and PVC apron advertising Worcester sauce. She looked a little taken aback at seeing P.C., but did as she was asked, and tried on the shoe. She looked ridiculous. I don't know how P.C. kept his face straight. Rubber gloves, PVC apron, old jeans of D.'s which were sizes too big for her, one blue striped trainer and one high-grade bendy perspex shoe. But it fitted.

We were then treated to one of those moments so beloved by movie makers, when time stands still for the principal protagonists while everyone else moves round about them. P.C. looked like a stunned tuna. C. went even more peculiar. She started to glitter. I thought it was just the sheen off the apron and possibly the shoe, but eventually she was completely suffused in glitter. And then she swanned off out of the door. Not a backward glance, or "Your lunch is in the oven," or anything at all.

C. is currently residing with P.C.'s mother until the nuptials. The excitement among the ordinary people at the unexpected turn of events is incomprehensible. They are hanging up bunting and organising street parties. I don't get it. I just don't get it.

D.'s turn to cook dinner. No wonder she was thrown out of finishing school. She has already set fire to a cabbage and blown up the toaster.

It is not raining today.

I don't think I'll bother keeping a diary.

I FIND IT ALL A LITTLE BIT FRIGHTENING

Linda McLean

I can feel my palms start to sweat and slide around within one another on my lap. When I look up my eyes blink too often. Piss off why don't you all piss off and leave me be. I don't say it. It would move me onto their ground. They won't get me that way.

Their faces are like crystal balls; all their little feelings coming and going. Jabby little faces — all hidden crevices, no open ground. They chip away, trying this technique, then that device. If they can't get through I'm a lost case.

I'm not lost. I'm safe. I'm alone. No holds, no pleasing, no otherness. Me, all the way through. They hate that. Not playing the game, playing my part. No function. Useless.

She's useful. Useful to him, to us, to her own mother. She bends, willing, will-less. She's a sorry tired woman with no real face left on her. A victim. She's been got at by everyone. Nobody's fault, she'll say. She'll not pounce on you. It's her lot.

Not mine. I didn't want it. I had no other way out. They played the game. I just didn't have it in me. I always wanted to run but couldn't. I wasn't a fighter.

I tried to play the game; the razor's edge. Playing, joking, laughing on the top, higher up. I was afraid to make a mistake. I was going to trip up and get caught out one of these days. Go underground. When the icy fear came and breathing made me dizzy, I went. I had gone. It's not so loud or frightening. Threats are meaningless.

It throws me out sometimes. You couldn't tell, but I know. I get hot, prickly, sticky. My mind races, jumping, darting. I'm good at hiding it, you'd never guess, but it makes me nervous. Maybe there's something I don't know. A trick to keep me out. It's not safe up there and I'm glad to get back.

I've seen things. Special things. A beautiful young girl lying dead in the sun took me away for days. I had to keep going back. She was trying to tell me something. I wanted to see if she was as beautiful as I remembered: the sunlight pulling up the golden threads in her hair; life, caught and stilled in those eyes; and her arms outstretched against the grass, embracing the sky. I want her to stay.

I could get out for ever if I really wanted. I could. I might even, when no-one is looking. I might just get up and go as suddenly as I arrived.

HAPPY FAMILIES

Janette Walkinshaw

I was sitting on the roof when this police car drove up and two policemen dragged me down and took me to the station. It was all right because the sergeant there knows me and knew it had just been a misunderstanding. He let me sleep in one of the cells since I couldn't be bothered walking all the way back to my digs. I'd like to know who it was 'phoned the police anyway. I asked the wife the next day and she said it wasn't her, because she hadn't noticed I was sitting on the roof. It must have been one of the neighbours who hadn't recognised me and thought I was a burglar. I thought it was a cheek myself because if a man can't sit on the roof of the house that is really his, even though the lawyer and the council made him, that is to say me, sign it over to my wife, without some interfering neighbour sending for the police then it's not a free country any more, that's all I can say.

I was there because I was wanting to speak to my wife's new husband as I had a business proposition to put to him. I was willing to overlook the unseemly haste with which she had encumbered herself with him because they are all at it now. They write a wee letter to the judge telling a lot of lies about their husband and the judge writes back and says all right, hen, you're divorced and the next day they belt down to the registry office and get themselves a new one. It's not the sort of thing you find a man doing. I said that to my wife when I went to see her and her new man with a crystal decanter which I gave them for a wedding present.

It doesn't matter what the judge said, I told her, if I was a catholic you'd still be married to me. It wouldn't matter whether you were a catholic or not she said I wouldn't still be married to you for anything and anyway it only counts if it's me that is the catholic. Exactly I said. That's the trouble with women. They will argue with you but they have no sense of logic and can't follow through a reasoned discussion. Her new man just sat and didn't say anything. I had taken the precaution of filling the decanter with half a bottle of whisky because I knew my wife would be unlikely to have anything in as she is dead against the drink, and we all had a glass or two. At least her new husband only had one and he sat and held it as if it was going to bite him. I wasn't surprised because it turned out he worked in an office, which to my mind is only a suitable place for wee lassies to work in.

I told him about the time I was in Saudi Arabia and I could see he was impressed. I would still be there as a matter of fact if the manager hadn't had it in for me because I was so good at the job and he was afraid if he went on leave I would get his job and he would be told not to come back, which was very likely as he was the kind of manager who took spites against his good employees and didn't stand by his men when they were in trouble. Of course it was in his interests that I was deported but I am not saying it was him told the Arabs I had a few bottles on me. How they expect a man to work in that heat without a refreshment beats me. Of course a man like my wife's new husband wouldn't understand that sort of thing, never having done anything more adventurous than sit behind a desk and write receipts.

I got a bit excited because telling them reminded me of the disgust I felt at the company at the time and I thumped the table to emphasize how unjust the whole thing had been, and unfortunately the decanter fell off the table and broke, which was a pity, but no great loss as I had finished the whisky that was in it. It wasn't really crystal anyway but just a glass one that I had picked up at the barrows.

To show there were no hard feelings because my wedding present had been broken I visited them regularly after that. I dropped in two or three times a week. It didn't matter if they were out because I still had a key to the front door so I could let myself in, and wait for them to come home. Sometimes they were awfully late and if they had been to the pictures they must have had a long romantic walk afterwards. I used to kid them about it, and they pretended to be annoyed. How they could afford to go out so often I don't know. My wife used to argue with me all the time about going out when I was only going down to the pub for a pint. She kept on about it, till you would think it was criminal, but now with her new man she was out gallivanting all the time.

HAPPY FAMILIES

When they were first married right enough they didn't go out much, so they were always in when I went to see them. They sometimes had the television on and didn't hear me at the door, but if I had left the key on my other key ring I just banged and shouted till they heard me. Bet you weren't actually watching television, I used to say, doing something more interesting that you couldn't come to the door. Her new man got awfully red in the face. It was a laugh right enough to see him so embarrassed.

When I left the police station I went round to ask my wife why the key hadn't fitted in the lock the previous night, but of course she explained that she had changed the locks because there had been burglaries in the street and she had lost her keys and she was scared the burglar would find them, so that was all right. I told her what I thought of the person who had reported me to the police for sitting on my own roof, and she asked me what I was doing on the roof anyway so I explained I was trying to get in and talk to her new husband. I was surprised they hadn't heard me, but she said they both slept sound.

Anyway it wasn't worthwhile going back to my digs so I just stayed there all day until her husband came in from his work that night. He was very surprised to see me there, as well he might because he knows I am a busy man and haven't the time to hang about waiting for him.

While our wife gave us our tea I put it to him straight that he was wasting his time working in an office for peanuts when he could come into business with me. All it needed was a little bit of capital and unfortunately my capital was all tied up in sound investments for long term growth so if he could see his way to raising a hundred pounds to buy stock with we would be on our way and nothing to stop us becoming another Marks and Spencer. I could see he was very enthusiastic but the wife kept butting in and telling him to have nothing to do with it, which I thought was very unfair and shortsighted. After all, I said to her, she was the one that used to complain when I was between jobs and had no security, and here was I offering her new man a chance to become self-employed and independent. I would have told her just to shut her mouth, but I didn't because I reckoned it was not my place to do so, in the circumstances, and up to her new man.

I couldn't persuade him to invest any money right away so I invited both of them to the barrows the next Sunday to see my new business in operation.

As luck would have it, it was a foul day that Sunday, and I couldn't display the stock to its best advantage on account of having to keep it under cover. It did clear up a bit about ten o'clock so I spread the computers out on the board in front of the stall and started my spiel to attract the customers of which there were a few about, even in the rain.

I saw a boy with his dad and gave them the sales talk about this new micro-computer which was only £4.99 and a bargain at that, educational and would help the kid get his highers. I was showing them how it worked when the wean stuck his fingers into it and god knows how he managed it but couldn't get his hand out again, for it was jammed in between the data bank recorder and the wee button you press to make the lights flash, and he was yelling blue murder. I said to his dad that in the circumstances I would only charge £3.99 and the man said he was damned if he would and it was only a bit of plastic anyway, so we started arguing. My wife and her new man chose that minute to turn up though I didn't see them right away on account of I had just punched the man for saying I was drunk which was a dirty lie. The punch only landed on his shoulder, which I did deliberately on account of not wanting to hurt him, but he started shouting that he was going to send for the police and charge me with assault. I said I would charge him with theft if his kid didn't give me back the computer terminal, and he wrenched it off the wean's hand and threw it at me. In the circumstances I considered it expedient to pretend the incident was over, and anyway it had started to rain again and all the merchandise was getting wet.

I was getting a bit fed up with the whole thing by this time because I had only sold a cassette at twenty two pence, and the man in the pub that sold me the stall and told me it was a cushy number was a liar, that's the kindest thing I can say about him. Just then anyway the man that collects the rent for the barrows came round and said I had no right to be there on account of every stall needed permission when it changed hands which I hadn't got. He said he wouldn't have me within ten miles of the place, which I could not understand, but thinking about it now I suppose he was acquainted with the manager in Saudi Arabia and had been listening to lies about me.

I just walked away as it seemed the best thing to do, especially as the wife and her new man were standing watching.

I went round to see them that night. They didn't hear me at the door so I shouted to make them hear and just kept on banging. He must have been awfully deaf right enough. I know the wife doesn't know what's what and is so wrapped up in herself anyway she wouldn't notice if the moon fell down, but you would think with him working in an office he would be alert, but it took an awful lot of shouting to bring him to the door. He stood on the step and his mouth was opening and shutting, but I couldn't make out what he was saying because I was feeling a bit tired by this time, so I pushed past him and went into the house and lay down on the couch.

I supposed I must have fallen asleep because the next thing I knew I was in the ambulance on the way here, which was a surprise because I didn't know I was ill.

So here I am in this hospital where the nurses treat you quite well though one of the doctors has got hold of the wrong end of the stick and keeps saying I would be well if I gave up the whisky. He's black and doesn't understand what whisky is on account of they don't have it where he comes from. I just agree with him because it seems a shame not to and it makes him that pleased.

I was hearing, actually, just the other day that the wife's new man is away from her, and that suits me fine, because I have decided to leave here and go back and live with her. Whether we get married again or not I will make up my mind about depending on how she behaves herself. I'll be leaving here any day now, but I won't let her know I'm coming. I'll just arrive. She will be pleased.

*

SNAKES AND LADDERS

Dilys Rose

Lily picked at the hem of her coatsleeve while she waited. She was wearing her good coat today — at least, it used to be good but now it was fraying at the cuffs. Since Sammy went into hospital she had been losing weight and her clothes, as well as being shabby, drooped over her narrow shoulders. It didn't seem worth cooking a proper dinner just for one, and besides, skipping meals saved money. Not that there was ever any to save.

The waiting room smelled of disinfectant, like the hospital. The doctors there told her, when she could get hold of one of them, that Sammy was making "some improvement" but she didn't notice any. The therapist said that Sammy was interested in clay and had him throwing fistfuls of it at the wall. Something about frustration, the therapist had said, but there was more to it than that. Everyone in her area must be frustrated if frustration meant throwing things. There were broken windows all over. Sammy would be normal if that was all there was to it. They were giving him drugs to "regulate his behaviour", that's what they said, but the drugs just made him talk a lot of nonsense or loll around with his mouth hanging open. He was like a lump of clay himself on those sedatives. He still screamed if anyone mentioned a cupboard. One day he threw himself at the wall.

"Number eight, please." A thin woman got up, tugging at the man next to her. He grunted, heaved to his feet and slouched after her through the door marked 'INTERVIEWS'. The door clicked shut. Lily's plastic card had '9' on it so she would be next. She bit a ragnail

62

and fixed her eyes on a poster directly opposite her. There was nothing else to look at. At least in the hospital there were some old magazines which other visitors had left behind. She crushed her coat lapels together. She didn't seem to be able to feel warm these days, no matter what the temperature.

In large black letters the poster commanded:

TAKE PRIDE IN YOUR ENVIRONMENT —
DON'T SPOIL IT WITH LITTER.

The words were printed on a stretch of very green grass, sprinkled with daisies: right in the middle of the meadow lay a pile of crisp packets and broken beer bottles. Who'd want to spoil such lovely grass? Lily couldn't remember seeing grass which looked as green. Your environment, that's where you stay, your area. There was nothing in the poster which looked at all like Lily's area except the litter but even that looked wrong. It was too clean, as if it had been put there for the picture. You could sweep that up in a minute. Litter, as Lily knew it, meant streets of rotting filth which spewed out of the drains every time it rained and crawled further and further up the walls of the flats. And the grass wasn't green, like that. It was nearer the colour of dishwater.

"Number nine, please." The number eight people slammed the waiting room door behind them as they left. Lily went into the interview room, holding out her number. The young clerk coughed briskly into his fist, then scraped his chair forward until he was tucked in tightly behind his desk. He began thumbing through a pile of forms. Lily smiled, noticing that his shirt was missing a button. Needs looking after, she thought, just like Sammy.

"Now then, your name is Marsh, Lily Marsh, is that correct?" The clerk spread his arms across the polished wood and leaned towards Lily. She nodded in reply.

"And you're divorced Mrs Marsh, am I right? And reside at 125 Hill View, 14/B, Easter Drumbeath?"

"Yes."

"And I understand you've applied for a transfer?"

"I want to move to another area."

The clerk pulled a green form from the pile. It was a dull colour, a bit like the doors on the flats at her end of Hill View, where you couldn't see the hills. You could see the quarry though, a great lake of yellow mud. The council had re-painted the doors on the other end of the street a year past, but they'd stopped halfway. Something to do with the government, she'd heard.

"You see, my son's in the hospital, he had a terrible shock . . ." At this moment the clerk was overwhelmed by a fit of sneezing and, fumbling to find a handkerchief, knocked most of his forms to the floor. Lily picked them up and returned them to the table while the young man blew his nose and pressed his fingers into his eyes.

"You should be in your bed," said Lily. The clerk coughed then gave her a bleary smile.

"Yes I . . . no, I'm afraid some of us must keep going," he replied as though remembering a motto. He straightened up his papers.

"Now, can we go through this step by step, Mrs Marsh?" He glanced at the clock while he spoke. "You say your son resides with you . . ."

"Yes, he stays with me, but we can't go on staying where we are. That's why Sammy's in the hospital." The clerk sighed, stubbing his pencil agains the desk. He took a deep breath.

"I'm aware that Easter Drumbeath is not the most desirable housing area but there's a long list for houses anywhere. Easter Drumbeath houses forty thousand tenants and I would say, at a modest estimate, twenty per cent of the householders have applied for a transfer within the last five years. Do you know how many people that is, Mrs Marsh? Eight thousand at least!" The clerk spread his arms wide. Lily shrank back from him, feeling very small and wishing she had someone there to help her say her piece.

"I know it's hard for other people in Drum," she said. "The place is in a terrible state. It's like," her fingers twisted into her cuffs, "like the inside of a litter bin."

"Ah . . . but you see, the council cannot be held responsible for litter. After all, who drops the litter?"

"It's not just that," Lily began but the clerk had his eye on the clock.

"I must explain to you that the council allocates rehousing through what we call a point system." He raised his eyes to the ceiling as though he were trying to remember his lines. "This is based on the present condition of the tenant's housing. I must emphasise that the waiting list is extremely long and, in all fairness I feel, would be better closed for the time being. Even if your points do add up to the required number, it is likely to be a considerable time before the relocation takes place. With the situation as it is, it might be better not to raise people's hopes. Do you see what I mean, Mrs Marsh?"

The clerk peered at Lily with such weary eyes that she felt obliged to nod, although she wanted to ask about the point system and relocation and how long a "considerable time" was likely to be. But she didn't want to be a nuisance.

"Let's start with you, Mrs Marsh. Do you work?"

"No."

"What about your ex-husband. Does he provide any maintenance?"

Lily answered the first batch of questions to the top of the clerk's head while he ticked off boxes on the green form.

"I have a note here to the effect that you are behind with your rent payments."

"It's only three weeks behind," she replied. "It's the first time. You see my son's in hospital and the new payment scheme's not working properly yet."

"There was a circular, Mrs Marsh, supplying advance information concerning the delay. You were advised to make alternative arrangements."

Lily had received the letter but she couldn't make alternative arrangements. She couldn't borrow money. Who was there to borrow from? No one she knew had money to spare and the pawn wouldn't give her anything for her belongings. The bus fares to the hospital. They added up. And the cups of tea in the café. She made them last longer by letting them stand until they were almost cold. That way she could spend more time in the cafe and avoid the house, what was left of it, a bit longer.

"Still," said the clerk, "I imagine many people in Easter Drumbeath are in the same position. We'll try to find out what can be said in your favour. You see, if you are lacking in some basic amenities like a clean water supply or electricity, it will be easier to push a transfer through."

"They're going to cut of my elecricity soon. I can't pay the bill." Lily hadn't intended to mention the electricity but the clerk seemed to be saying that having it cut off would help in some way.

"I'm afraid I can't help you on that count. You see, if it had already been cut off, it might have made a difference but we can only take the present situation into consideration."

"But the flats are damp," Lily replied. "I've got to keep the fire on all the time. There's damp all over the walls, in big black patches." The clerk took a note of this. The word "damp" was given a tick. One point to Lily. It was if the two were playing a strange game of snakes and ladders, with Lily landing on more than her fair share of snakes. When the clerk reached the bottom of the third page of questions, there remained a small space without any boxes.

"Now, are there any particular circumstances you'd like to mention in the 'comments' section?" Lily's knuckles had gone white from clenching her fingers inside the palms of her hands. She had been trying to tell the clerk about Sammy from the beginning and now there was just this little space left without any boxes.

"He had a breakdown, my son Sammy. He had a terrible shock and then he had a breakdown." She paused, wondering whether there would be room for any more.

"Go on, Mrs Marsh."

"There was this empty flat . . . . on the floor below. Sammy used to go in there sometimes to . . . just to look around, for something to do . . ." She couldn't say that he brought her the floorboards for firewood. "He was poking around, just looking at things. He'd told me about a funny smell coming from a cupboard. I said it would just be the damp because everything smells rotten when it's damp. The cupboard was locked. I said he shouldn't force it, I told him to leave well alone but you know what kids are like. He got the door open and there he was!"

"Who was, Mrs Marsh?"

"Mr Martin, from flat eleven, hanging from a rope, poor man. There were . . . things moving all over him. Poor Sammy, poor Mr Martin, I'm sorry!" Lily choked to a halt.

The young man was embarrassed by the weeping woman in front of him but he had come across this kind of thing before. Sometimes it was just a put-on.

"So, ah . . . this breakdown you say your son had, this would have occurred as a result . . . of the shock of seeing this . . . corpse?" Lily lowered her head. "I do sympathise with you Mrs Marsh, I'll try to do what I . . . ." The clerk's condolences were cut short by another insuppressible sneeze.

*   *   *

Lily walked home along the canal. It was a long walk but it helped pass the time. It was a bright day and the sun stroked the back of her neck like a warm fingertip. Towards the end of the landscaped walkway, she began to start noticing the litter. A piece of broken bottle had trapped the sun on its curve and shone fiercely. A wisp of smoke curled round the jagged edge. Below the glass,. the weeds were scorched.

Lily climbed through the torn fence where Easter Drumbeath's tangle of cement walkways snaked across the motorway. This was where the gardens abruptly came to an end, where the birdsong petered out. In Drumbeath the birds didn't stay long except the scavenging gulls: and they didn't sing, they squawked.

She glanced back at the neat bungalows and their well-tended lawns. She'd always wanted a garden, a small one would do fine, a lawn set off with a blaze of colour in the flower-beds. But they'd never give her a garden. On the path, the broken bottle had started a small fire. How easy that would be, she thought. She had heard of folk who did such things.

When she arrived at the centre, she counted out her change and stopped at one of the few shops which wasn't an off-licence or a betting-shop. A row of fortresses, grilled and barred with iron. No-one wanted a shop here anymore, the insurance was too high, the break-ins were too frequent, even with their iron bars and electronic alarms. She pushed open the heavy door.

The man behind the counter was filling in a pools coupon and smoking between coughs. On the counter lay a pile of shrivelled oranges next to slabs of sausage meat and discoloured bacon. The radio crackled out a song about the bright city of somewhere else.

"Yeah?" he said, without looking up.

"How much is a gallon of paraffin?" Lily asked, as casually as possible.

FELLOW TRAVELLERS

Agnes Owens

Jean boarded the train standing in the station and pulled on the sliding door of the empty compartment. It was stiff and hard to move but she wanted a few moment's privacy to assemble her thoughts. She settled down in the corner and opened her bag to take out cigarettes then changed her mind. Her throat was as rough as sandpaper with the concentrated smoking of the morning. She peered through the smeared window. The platform clock conveyed there was still five minutes before the train left. Now she was undecided. Should she go back? Perhaps she had acted hastily. She rose and heaved upon the compartment door again. As she stood wondering, the electrically controlled outer doors of the train slid shut. She pressed on the button, but they held fast. It was disgraceful. How were people to get in or out. She banged on the window, but the platform was deserted. The doors opened and she was confused again. To return now was to admit defeat. She went back to her corner. To her chagrin in came a man and woman of advanced years. They dithered in the doorway of the compartment. The woman smiled at Jean. Jean's eyes dropped. Subdued, they settled for the seat adjacent, and spoke to each other in whispers. Then the whistle blew like a sigh of relief.

Just before the outer doors closed a man hurtled through the compartment and threw himself at the seat opposite Jean, breathless and unpleasantly close. He bumped her knee. "Sorry," he leered. She had a quick impression of dark hair and brown eyes. Before she could draw her breath he had thrust a packet of cigarettes towards her. Hypnotised by his forcefulness she took one. With similar speed he produced a lighter and held it under her nose.

"Damned cold," he stated with a cigarette dangling from his lips. He leaned back and crossed his legs. The tip of his shoe prodded her calf.

She nodded and withdrew her leg. His gaze veered over to the couple then back.

"I'm bloody frozen," he said confidentially.

He shivered in an exaggerated way and blew his free hand. She took an instant dislike to him, but what was worse she suspected he had been drinking. The prospect of being confined with this person for the half hour's journey was daunting, but to move away seemed drastic. Besides she was smoking his cigarette.

"The weather's bloody awful," he complained.

She grunted something unintelligible. Her throat was dry and her tongue fired with smoke.

"Going to the city?" he asked.

"Not exactly." She considered getting off at the next stop, but then she would be landed in a village with nothing to offer except the Railway Hotel.

"I'm going to see my brothers," he confided. "City lads."

"I don't care for the city," she said, hoping to put him in his place.

"City folk are the best." His eyes were bold and disturbing. The old couple were staring openly at them.

She backed down. "I've nothing against city people."

He leaned forward. "My family come from the city — great people." He added, "And my father was born in the city. He's been dead for ten years."

He sighed. Jean's eyes were glazed with apathy.

"Do you know," he said pointing his finger, "they had to hold me back in the hospital when they told me he'd snuffed it. One of the best, he was."

"H'mm," said Jean.

"He gave us everything. It wasn't easy, mind you." He shook his head sadly, and ground his cigarette end into the floor creating a black smear near her shoe. The train sped through the start of the built up area. Jean tried to calculate the stops ahead of her.

Unthinkingly she took out her cigarettes, then felt obliged to offer him one. He took it without saying thanks.

"I could get off at any stop and I would be sure to meet a relative." He smirked and added, "Where are we anyway?"

They gazed through the window to multi-storey flats flashing by.

"My uncle lives up there somewhere," he said.

"Fancy," she said, looking out to a field of cows.

"Do you remember Dickie Dado, the footballer?"

She lied. "Uh huh."

"He was my nephew — great player wasn't he?"

"Er — yes. I don't know much about football though." She gave a depreciating giggle.

He glared at her. "He died two years ago. Surely you know that."

"I'm sorry. I don't know." Jean's face reddened.

"The team was never the same."

He looked over at the old couple and raised his voice.

"To think he died at twenty three and some of these old fogeys go on forever."

Jean pulled hard on her cigarette. The old man stiffened. She concentrated on the view but she could feel her companion's eyes probing through her skin.

"You wouldn't think I've got a great family of my own — would you?"

She was forced to confront his sly smile.

"No. I mean, have you?"

"Two girls and a boy. Marvellous kids."

The information angered her. "So what?" she wanted to scream. Then to add to her misery the train increased its speed and caused them to bump up and down together in a ridiculous fashion. She pressed herself back against the compartment wall as he lurched about slackly, giving off a sour smell of alcohol. Her cigarette fell from her fingers and rolled about the floor. Mercifully the bumping stopped. Jean wiped the sweat from her forehead.

He began again. "The wife says I shouldn't show any favouritism. She thinks because I bought the boy a fishing rod he's my favourite. It's not true you know." His eyes pleaded for justice. Jean thought she would detest brown eyes forever.

To stop his flow of words she began in desperation, "I've got a headache, would you mind — "

He appeared not to hear her.

"I bought the girls a teaset," he interrupted. "You should see them with it. They make me drink tea out of the wee cups — simply marvellous." He shook his head overcome at the image.

"I see," said Jean letting her breath out slowly. Her eyes wavered towards the couple who were whispering intently. She pulled herself together and stated in a loud voice, "I find families a complete bore."

"Never," he said, taken aback for the first time. "The trouble with people nowadays is they don't care enough about their families. Pure selfishness that's what's wrong with everyone."

He looked over to the old couple for support but they were staring ahead with blank expressions.

He went on, "Take my girls, they're just great, and the boy as well. Mind you I don't show any favouritism — the wife's wrong, but she can be a bitch at times." His lips curled and he repeated, "a pure bitch."

"If your kids are so wonderful, why didn't you take them with you," Jean snapped and looked upwards to verify the situation of the communication cord.

He spread his hands out and whined, "The wife wouldn't let me. I told you she's a pure bitch."

Jean felt worn out. The train was slowing down for the next stop.

"I think this must be Duntrochen," she mumbled, toying with the idea of getting off.

"Not this place," he said with authority.

As the train pulled out she spied the notice board.

"It was Duntrochen," she accused, and closed her eyes to avoid any further involvement. Her eyelids flickered as his leg brushed against hers. She was obliged to move. Her companion was staring over the top of her head when she faced him with fury. To sever all contact she turned to the woman sitting beyond.

"Very tiring these train journeys," she gabbled. The woman looked startled.

"Y-yes," she stammered.

"I was really intending to get off at Duntrochen," Jean added hoping to establish a safe relationship with the dreary pair.

"It's a one-eyed hole anyway," her brown-eyed companion stated in his outrageous way.

Jean was consumed with hatred, but she was trapped into answering, "That's a matter of opinion."

"My mother died in Duntrochen hospital."

Jean was prepared to sneer at this disclosure, but the couple were looking at him with concern.

"That's enough to put you off any place," the woman replied.

"She was a wonderful person. Brought up ten of us without any complaint."

The couple · nodded with understanding. Jean pictured with detestation a family album portraying a white haired woman with ten leering faces looking over her shoulder.

"She couldn't do enough for us," his voice jarred on.

Jean coughed and began searching in her handbag. Anything to distract her from the creeping weight of his words.

"Mind you, she liked her drink now and then."

The couple were definitely attracted by this news. Their eyes blinked rapidly as the image of the saintly mother changed to one of a boozy hag.

"It was her only pleasure."

"Amen," said Jean under her breath.

But the subject was not finished. He touched her knee and said, "He was never off her back, my old man."

For a hideous moment she thought he was making a sexual innuendo.

"Gave her a life of hell," he added.

"Oh you mean," Jean spoke in relief, "a kind of persecution —"

The woman tutted. Her husband looked ill at ease. Jean rejoiced at their discomfort.

"Not surprising," she said, addressing the couple.

Her companion gave her a hard look, but he let the remark pass, and stated, "She was one of the best, that's what I say."

"But," said Jean, determined now to expose his inanity, "you told me your father was one of the best."

"That's right," he replied, defiant.

"Now you say he gave your mother a life of hell and she was the best. I don't follow you." She bestowed a knowing smile on the old couple, but they looked at her uncomprehendingly.

"She never complained," he said with the quiet triumph of one who holds the ace card.

Jean wiped her clammy hands on her skirt. She figured she could be on the verge of a nervous breakdown. The word valium came into her head. Her friend Wilma took valium pills regular and she was in charge of a typing pool. They must work wonders. She decided to get off at the next stop, no matter where it was, and head for the nearest chemist. She stood up and tugged at the compartment door.

"What's the hurry," he called, but she was transfixed by the thought that she might have to get a doctor's prescription for vallium. As the train pulled up she was flung back almost on top of the woman.

"Are you all right?" the woman asked with concern.

"Yes," said Jean, pulling down her skirt. To justify her erratic behaviour she explained, "I thought I was going to be sick. I haven't felt well all morning."

"I see," said the woman darting a considerate glance in the direction of Jean's stomach. Jean shot up like a jack-in-the-box. A tic beat on her cheek and her mouth twitched.

"I must get out of here," she chattered.

"Don't upset yourself." The woman tugged on her arm. Her grip was surprisingly strong.

Jean fell back on the seat. She explained in a heightened manner, "Not morning sickness — just ordinary average sick."

The woman patted her hand. Jean rounded on her with venom. "I'm not even married."

The couple regarded each other with dismay. The brown-eyed man blew smoke through his nostrils.

"Of course," said Jean, forcing herself to be calm, "I think you are all off your rockers."

"Really," said the old man. His wife shook her head as if in warning. The other man continued to blow smoke like streams of fury.

"I thought it was bad enough listening to that looney," she gestured towards the other man, "but you two appear to be in your dotage."

The couple cowered close to the window. The man tapped his head significantly.

"Thank goodness I'm getting off here," Jean uttered wildly and charged out the compartment. She alighted from the train without a clue to where she was.

"Ticket please," said the collector when she scuttled through the barrier. "Always have your ticket ready," he reproved as she fumbled in her bag.

She moved out of the station in a distraught manner. She hesitated, torn between the beckoning brightness of Woolworth's and a telephone box on the opposite pavement. She braced herself and headed for the box. She dialled a number and held the receiver to her ear. Almost immediately the voice spoke. She cut through the querulous preamble.

"It's me — Jean. I'm sorry I rushed out like that —" She paused to listen as the voice gained strength. "I know mother," she replied wearily, "but you must understand I have to get out sometime for a bit of relaxation. I won't be doing anything desperate. After all I'm not a teenager."

Her reflection in the stained mirror on level with her eyes verified the statement, showing the marks of the crow's feet.

The voice began again like the trickle of a tap. Jean interrupted.

"Yes mother I'm fine. I won't be gone forever you know. I'll be back around tea time."

She replaced the telephone and stood for a moment within the box feeling she had placed herself beyond mercy. In retrospect the man with the brown eyes became desirable. He had spoken to her and touched her knee. In his inept way he had offered her an association. She should have been flattered if not actually grateful and really he had not been all that bad-looking. It would have been something to boast about to her friend Wilma, who according to herself was continually exposed to such encounters. As she stepped out of the telephone box the memory of her neurotic outburst engulfed her in shame. She walked along the pavement, head downwards, hunched against the cold — going nowhere.

THINKING ABOUT MARRIAGE

Rhiannon Williams

This large-boned young woman is sitting on a wooden jetty in the sun with her feet in the water. Her skin is slightly red, slightly gold and is soft. Her eyelids are creased; the blue that shows, clear. On three sides of her, lake-water gleams. Behind, rough wood stretches to the land.

Having thought carefully, not decisively, it is time to leave. The soles of her feet wet the planks; her leg muscles ache slightly; skin surfaces touch, damp, hot, through thin cotton — backs of legs, breasts, knees — and her hands rest on the wood for a second longer than necessary.

She stands, swaying slightly in the heat, puts her hand to her temple and, beginning to walk to the shore, she feels her pulse.

Her head is then in shade and there are cold pine-needles between her toes and now in her sandals.

In the fields behind the village she will meet a friend. She will wriggle her toes and they will laugh about this feeling. They will hug and part. One of them will look back.

Before they meet again, space and support will be found in a masculine embrace, and work will be done.

MOONRUNNING

Mary McCabe

Three faces.

The woman with the bun-shaped face, soft jowls, social smile.

The smug man in the winged armchair, arched eyebrows, thick lips, long scraggy throat with throbbing lump.

The adolescent with the knock knees, gangling before the fireplace with his socks beyond his trousers and his chin a-pock with red.

"Come in, come in, my dear!"

"If you don't mind my saying so, you look even prettier than you did in the picture."

"Do sit down! Would you like tea or coffee? Barry, put the kettle on for your little friend!"

"My goodness, your English is good. If Barry had learnt French to that standard, he would be at university right now and our worries would be over."

"If you come upstairs, dear, I'll show you your room. Did you have a good flight?"

Clean little room with a sloping ceiling. Houseproud bed with soft sweet sheets. Pink flock carpet with little cardboard squares under the furniture legs. Glass-topped dressing-table with fussy frilly mats. Welcoming wide window for when the dreams come and the wind calls over the autumn fields.

"Milk or lemon?"

"Tell us about your homeland. You live in the country, don't you?"

"Perhaps the young people would like to go out for a walk afterwards. I'm sure Barry would be glad to show Lucia around our woods."

"For Christ's sake, Dad! You always make it sound so suggestive!"
"I should warn you, Lucia. Our Barry is a flower. His shell-like ears
redden before impurity."
"Lay off, can't you! I don't want to be like you."
Brown needles below, trunks ascendant. A Forestry Commission
project and nothing primeval or deciduous about it. Warm, sweaty
soft palm clutching, spaniel eyes glancing.

"Did you sleep well? Barry's still in his pit, the lazy . . . Barry!"
"I'm afraid the weather's not so good today, dear. What are your
plans?"
A silver wet village, each stone with its part. As genes build the
cells which declare the species, so these sandstones make only a
Scottish High Street, quite unlike the low yellow cottages of the
seaside Danes, the bright Lego blocks of Aegean waters, the planned
prettiness of German suburbia. An old, run-down land, but new to
me. Tonight would be one of them. A small warm glow, exciting in
its secrecy, astounding in its reality.
"Hello, Mrs Drysdale. Have you met Lucia? Lucia Grenier."
"So this is Barry's pen-friend! I've heard a lot about you. Do you
speak English . . . ? Of course, silly me. It's a pity about the weather,
isn't it? You're not getting a very good impression of the place?"
Round cushion faces on plump perfumed necks. Thin nosy faces
on crepey wrinkled necks. Dirty pitted faces on stubbly necks.
Tonight.

"I thought you might want to stay up with Barry to watch the
thriller."
"Should be good, Lucia. It's got Charles Bronson."
"How romantic. Just the fellow to fire a young maid's passion."
"Can it, Dad. How about it then? Are you sure?"
Cool smooth sheets. On the ceiling, the flash of sharks' teeth.
Night drivers under the sky. Lonely lorries, sales saloons,
Dormobiles dreaming. Through the open window the night calling
and OUT! On the moist earth landing, running free, faster, faster.
Over the fence into the field, cutting a dash through the soft high
barley, a parting of the waving hair. The joy of this blind gallop, the
taste of the harvest air, the world in silver negative. Insects, field
mice, all flee from this wilder motion, irresistible surge. Out of the
blonde grass tumbles the stranger. Down a muddy lane, splish
splash, and on a bare hillside I call to the stars.
Down again at a hurtle, frisking, rolling. On the damp rock ribbon

cars, one, two, three. What surprise on the drivers' faces tonight! Then, as the firmament pales, the track winds home to the window, the pink flock carpet, polyester sheets.

"A pint of heavy, and two of lager."
"Look who comes here — better make it three."
"Hey, Barry, you look terrible! Aren't you getting enough sleep?"
"You're all right now, eh? Wouldn't mind coming back to that after a hard day signing on the buroo."
"Give me peace. It isn't like that. She's just a friend."
"You mean she's leading you on? Giving you the old headache treatment?"
"You're worse than Dad! I should have stayed at home."
"A Professor of Zoology ought to know about such things, wouldn't you say? Young love. Ah, when I recall my early days . . ."
"How did you meet her, anyway?"
"Yes, how was it? Tell us again about it. Frank doesn't know."
"Through the International Chums Club."
"The International . . . ha ha ha!"
"Next, you can join the Wolf Cubs!"
"I've had it. I'm off."
Silence.
"Poor guy. We shouldn't slag him, I suppose."
"He brings it on himself."
"Did you know this Lucia bird is his first?"
"Never. At his age? What about that . . . that . . . what was her name . . . Geraldine?"
"Never existed. All in his mind."
"Poor bloke."

The brows are down, the hooded lids lowered. Ivory and jet set in a carved stand from the Near East. The mouth is grim, the Adam's apple bobs.
"It's checkmate! By Jove, she's done it."
"How could you? David hates to be beaten. And by a girl!"
"Sylvia, that's unfair. I have always maintained that a well-trained woman is a match for any man. You can be proud of yourself, child. You have checkmated the Master of the Class of '52, and you don't look any the less pretty for it. Now, why don't you wenches take yourselves off into the kitchen and leave a man to his scars?"
"He won't forgive you for this, you know."
"Indeed I shall be avenged. What about after lunch tomorrow?"
"Sorry, sorry. Mustn't interrupt the course of true love."

I am fast. I am freedom. I am fantasy. Down by the loch where the trees wade deep in water and the reeds are bonny brown hair. Up in the mounds, rocks pimple through the turf. Such territory my strong legs cover. I am strength. I am power. I am the force that chases the shadows of the clouds.

Unpainted farm sheds, wood and corrugated iron in a scraped dirt yard. Through yellow windows, faces fix on a screen like flickering porridge. They grin at it. I grin at them. One grins at me. Racing round the back among old bins and barrels. Feathers, screeching, flapping. A stone hits me, and I slope for the moon.

"Why do you want to know about Scotland? I want to know about you, not your country. Let's sit on that wall. It looks dry. I suppose you've had quite a few boyfriends? Do you feel cold? There, is that better? You don't mind my holding you like this, do you?"

"No, not many. Just one or two, but none that lasted long. Let's talk about you, not me. What dainty ears you have — the shape of church windows. Could . . . do you mind if . . . oh, I'm sorry. I hope I didn't hurt your teeth?"

Glug, glug. Crimson the good wine falls down his gullet, past the dark blood pumping in the jugular, having fed his clever brain.

"Hey, Dad, this is up your street. Mr Gillespie . . ."

"Mr who?"

"Local farmer. He was disturbed by some unknown beast prowling about his yard. Apparently it frightened his son by appearing at the window, and then proceeded to invade the henhouse. 'At Mr Gillespie's approach, the creature left without inflicting any casualties amongst the chickens'."

" 'The creature'? 'Unknown beast'? What's the fellow talking about? Unknown to him, perhaps."

"He said it looked like a wild boar . . ."

"There have been no wild boar in Scotland for two hundred years."

". . . or perhaps a fat wolf."

"Last wolf in Scotland was killed in 1743."

"Or even a bear."

"The Caledonian bear has not been seen since 1057. It was probably a dog."

"Probably."

"Didn't someone recently try to reintroduce wolves into Scotland?"

"He was stopped and prosecuted."

"There's a bear park at Loch Lomond. Maybe one escaped."

"Sylvia. It was a dog. A dog!"

"What — are you going out now? It's nearly nine o'clock!"

"A young girl shouldn't wander alone at night. Why not take Barry with you?"

"Oh, Dad, I can't go out just now. The Clark Masterton show will be on in ten minutes."

"If you would shift yourself to get a summer job you would have money to buy video tapes to record the programmes you wish to see."

"If you were a normal decent parent you'd let me use your video tapes."

"My tapes are reserved for programmes I plan to keep."

"All of them? What about that one?"

"I refuse to argue the point. Lucia is your houseguest. If she wants to go for a walk you must escort her."

"Oh, very well . . . But look, Dad, she doesn't want to go out after all!"

Shouldn't wander . . . little did they know! Flashing over turf and mud, splashing through black wetness, dashing through empty streets! Three young drunks singing, long drawn out notes like the howls of an animal in sorrow. One tilts to the left, one to the right, so that the central drunk does not know which way to fall. A playful nip, perhaps to the neck or to the calf. Ah, what fun to see them scatter. The sober terror in their eyes, the disbelief! No one thinks me impudent now. The liberty of it!

"Why do you want to visit the Hebrides? Barren clumps of rock, by all accounts; not that I've been there myself."

"No, I'm originally a Home Counties man. Been here five years, but still miss the Smoke."

"Dad got offered this seat at the university, you see. Too good a chance to turn down."

"Not much. The parents have a pad down in Wales, to which they repair periodically, but I prefer a sunny place for a holiday."

"Seen Edinburgh, of course — haven't got around yet to Glasgow."

"Around three-quarters of a million — I believe it's lost half a million in the part thirty years. Do you mind if we stop talking about geography?"

"What? . . . Oh, yes, very nice view from here. Lucia, come closer."

"Your bone structure — something almost primeval — you don't at all have a twentieth century face! And such pointed, artistic little hands."

"How curious! Look, your ring finger is longer than your middle finger. Yes, it's the same on the other hand!"

"Really? You don't say."

"Lucia, I'm not interested in the courtship traditions of your home village. Let me show you ours . . . come here, you elusive thing, you!"

"Your father was called out on an unusual mission, today."

"Yes, the hospital wanted me to identify a couple of bites."

"Bites?"

"Extraordinary case. Two fellows last night, rather the worse for wear, were attacked by some creature they couldn't identify."

"But surely they saw it!"

"Between them, or, should I say among them, for they were accompanied by an unbitten friend — they had consumed at least fifteen double whiskies and umpteen pints of heavy!"

"Pass the *Radio Times*, Mum. I think there's a horror film on tonight."

"So what did bite them?"

"Do you know, I couldn't be sure!"

"*You* couldn't be sure?"

"The molars suggested a herbivore, but the large canines . . ."

"Were they badly injured?"

"Flesh wounds."

"Perhaps it was a vampire!"

"I knew your television addiction would claim you in the end!"

". . . or a werewolf!"

"Had it been a werewolf, surely they would have been badly mauled."

"Not so, Sylvia. It is a Hollywood myth that the werewolf of the legends was always vicious. For example there is a story of a French werewolf which rescued a sixteenth century abbot from hungry wildcats!"

"My goodness!"

"Not to mention a Huguenot werewolf which saved from drowning the Catholic sea-captain who had murdered the werewolf's wife!"

"You're so well-informed, David. Barry, don't you think your father is well-informed?"

"It's on the coffee-table behind you, Mum."

"In any case, why should it be a werewolf? The legends of all countries tell of people changing by magic into various beasts. Here in Scotland we have the silkie, while in India there was the weretiger, and in Africa the werecrocodile."

"That must have been a sight to see!"

"All these creatures changed species periodically. Then there were the half-and-halfs, the centaurs, the minotaurs, the god Pan . . ."

"And the *TV Times* too, please, Dad."

"You want to watch television tonight? Shame on you!"

"Don't you want to go out one last evening with Lucia before she leaves?"

"Here it is. 'Curse of the Mummy's Bandage'."

"Lucia, what do you think of our son's cultural preference?"

"Give it a rest, Dad. Mum, Channel Four."

"Do you find him witty and charming, Lucia? An attentive lover?"

"I said, that's enough!"

"Don't be afraid to speak your mind, child. Your opinion couldn't be lower than ours."

"Now look what you've done, Dad. You've scared her away. Come back down, Lucia!"

"Huh! The girl has no gumption, no character. In three weeks she has said nothing of interest to anyone. I've tried to bring her out of her shell . . ."

"Your father is willing to discuss any subject under the sun with her."

"You're being unfair. She's a foreigner, and still young. You scare her . . ."

"As I said, the girl has no spirit about her at all. She's a mouse!"

WALTER

Anne Downie

Walter was a little different from the rest of us. Captured for posterity in the faded school photograph, he somehow manages to surmount its imposed uniformity. He peers at the camera through a chink in the Elastoplast in which his battered wire spectacles seem to be almost entirely encased. Most of the boys appear to have marked this momentous occasion with a visit to the barber, but Walter's large shorn skull is living testimony to, not so much a haircut, as an investment.

It wasn't just his name, Walter Walenska, that set him apart. Every day during the interval break we all used to produce 'play-pieces' which conformed to some unwritten maternal code . . . an apple, a biscuit, or a piece and jam, but Walter used to munch a fairly familiar object which puzzled me by its size. It was very large and wafer thin. Because of the exotic nature of his surname I enquired if this object was some strange foreign delicacy.

"Naw, it's just a roll an' buhter," he answered, changing his mind and wiping his nose on the lapel of his jacket when he saw the degree of encrustation upon his sleeve.

I looked scornful. Buttered rolls, of the well-fired variety, were a regular feature of breakfast in our house. Or at least they had been, until my mother discovered that their appetising warmth was not due to the fact that they were fresh from the oven but rather that the confused and snuffling dairy cat performed a daily incubatory ritual as they lay invitingly on the breadboard. Despite the unusual flavour that this sometimes imparted I still knew a roll when I saw one and

Walter's piece bore little resemblance to any I'd eaten or Smoky had inadvertently baptised. Walter smiled his blinkered smile.

"I'll show you the morra," was all he said.

Next day Walter produced a brown paper bag from his jacket pocket. He opened it to reveal that it held an ordinary morning roll which he held aloft, with the flourish of a conjuror about to perform a major transformation. He returned the roll to the bag and after carefully positioning it under his posterior he started to bounce up and down on top of it. He stopped occasionally to intersperse a sort of grinding motion with his buttocks. When the teacher arrived Walter's acrobatics were curtailed but the roll remained trapped between his bottom, which was encased in his usual grimy shorts, and the desk.

When the bell rang for interval break, Walter gave a few final jumps and grinds and then released the bag and reverently placed it on the desk. He opened it with some difficulty since the paper had given way under the constant rear assault.

"Want a bite?" he asked.

Despite the fact that the roll was now almost large enough to feed the whole class we all declined his generous offer . . . all, that is, with the exception of Willie McGurk, who never refused anything and plagued everyone for the stumps of their apples. He would even demand a bit of the chewing gum which you'd had in your mouth for hours or a drink of your 'penny pop' without wiping the neck of the bottle with the palm of his hand, which was the recognised procedure carried out by his more fastidious classmates.

It was for the Christmas tree incident, however, that I really remember Walter. We were sitting happily in class up to our armpits in glue, making those endless paper chains which seemed to be an inevitable part of school tradition at Christmas. All the teacher's attention was directed towards separating Bernadette Dougan's pigtails which had been glued firmly together by the ever-industrious, constantly hungry Willie McGurk. Shouting to be heard above Bernadette's protesting screams, Walter suddenly asked, "Huv you goat a Christmas tree?"

"Yes," I answered proudly.

"Bet it's no' a real tree," he said scathingly.

I did not quite understand his meaning. It was a very real tree. My mother could vouch for that as she daily swept up the fine layer of pine needles from the living-room carpet before my baby brother, an embryonic Willie McGurk, could sample their delicacy.

"Bet you it's no' as big as mine," Walter persisted.

"How big is yours?" I questioned.

"Bigger than a three-storey building," he replied, with a disturbingly convincing air.

My tree, I had to admit, could not match one of such grandiose proportions, so I resorted to the best defence I knew — disbelief.

"You'll go to the bad fire for telling lies," I said.

Father Kelly, the old priest who visited our school from time to time, was forever giving us graphic descriptions of Hell which sent a thrill of horror round the whole class. The thought of roasting on an eternal spit was bound to make Walter confess to his lie.

"Cross my heart and hope to die," was his reply.

These words really shook me. Father Kelly had also spent some time outlining the spiritual folly of taking false oaths and I knew that Walter would not risk Divine retribution. He must be telling the truth.

"You can come hame wi' me an' see if efter school,"he said, a generous offer in the face of my disbelief.

That afternoon, my curiosity making me, for once, ignore my mother's rule that I come straight home, I decided to accompany Walter. We came out of school to find that the snow, which had been falling steadily for several hours, was now covering familiar objects in a white disguise. Walter's only protection against the elements was a long multi-coloured woollen scarf which had been lying unclaimed in the teacher's desk for months, due, no doubt, to the hideous nature of its colour scheme. He had reluctantly put it on at the teacher's insistence when she saw that he had no coat or hat and wore only sandshoes on his feet.

We walked past rows of tenement houses until we came to a large stretch of waste ground known locally as "Moll's Mire".

"This way," said Walter indicating a gap in the hedge which skirted the waste ground.

"I'm not allowed in there. It's full of swamps and tinkers and bad men."

He cut short my argument and gently pushed me through the opening.

"Don't worry, we're here," he said.

I looked round in surprise but could not see any sign of a house, merely an old broken-down army hut. Part of the roof was missing and a tarpaulin had been thrown over the gaping hole. A little boy of about two years of age was playing happily in the snow which was lying in drifts in front of the hut, his enjoyment making him quite oblivious to the biting cold.

"This is ma brother, wee Robert."

Walter picked the child up and kissed his grimy grinning little face.

The little boy ran off into the hut.

"You live in there?" I asked, incredulously.

"Aye," said Walter. "We're squatters."

I remembered, then, some older girls at school saying that Walter was a squatter. I had thought perhaps it referred to his place of birth or that his parents were of a different political persuasion from my own. So this is what it meant. I was thrilled.

"Where's your tree?" I enquired.

Taking me by the arm he led me to a little clearing behind the hut.

"Well, whit do you think of it?" he asked on hearing my sharp intake of breath.

"Isn't it a stoater?"

I had to agree with his description, for, in the clearing, grew the tallest fir tree I had ever seen. It had a light dusting of snow which sparkled far brighter than the tawdry lights with which my own tree at home was festooned. In fact, when I thought of my own Christmas tree which we had covered in strands of cotton wool in a pathetic imitation of snow, I felt a twinge of envy. Walter produced some crumpled paper chains from his pocket and, after removing a variety of objects of indeterminate origin which adhered to their surface, he generously allowed me to decorate the lower branches. Then we both stood back and gazed upwards in silent admiration.

A FINISHED PICTURE

Morelle Smith

The night I welcomed Pain was as miniscule or as flooded as any other. It was, of course, within Time, but the arrangements leading to or away from it were blurred and haphazard, neither meticulous nor jumbled, neither singular nor commonplace. It was not a denouement, neither was it one of a series as, for example, the third step from the bottom of the stairs. I say it was within Time, but that could just be because I like to feel comfortable among all these emanations of the strange and indecipherable. Time has a variety of landscapes and seasons, yet it is a concrete orientation, or as concrete as one can get, and all the more welcome for that. Something happened that made me see Pain in a different way. I saw its connection with things I usually liked to keep separate from it, things like pleasure and love and inspiration. There, among my holiest of holies, it fell into place. And so at home it seemed, that I welcomed it. And in the moment of welcome it changed countenance and substance. So I became more interested in the process of transformation than in definitions. That's how Pain lost its power over me.

Pain used to be such a frequent caller that I could hardly say I welcomed it. It got to be one I would try to avoid, in the way one does with a persistent neighbour who is forever turning up to ask for a cup of sugar, or a couple of spoonfuls of flour, some minute, irritating, ingratiating amount, as close to nothing as you could imagine, as if by paring down the amount, the request could also be pared down to make it seem so little that was asked for, so very little, that it would be utterly churlish to refuse, yet the smaller the amount requested, the larger, somehow, seems the request, because the greater is the emphasis put on it, the heavier, somehow, the burden of giving it.

I had a neighbour like that once, and I came to dread the knock on the door. I had decided to go and live in a completely unknown city, where I knew no one, where I hoped to find the privacy and anonymity accorded to a complete stranger in a foreign country, speaking only a few words of the language. But it was just my luck to run into someone in the market whose tortured rendition of the language made plain her alien origins and whose distress prompted me to speak to her. Her relief — which I presumed was at finding someone who spoke English — was so intense that it carried her back along the street with me, and I discovered that my privacy had already ended, within two days and just across the street, there were its boundaries. From then on, my sojourn became a battle to keep this woman at bay, for her hunger for contact drove her quite beyond the bounds of good manners or good sense, or even friendship, had we been friends, which we were not, though perhaps she embraced in her conception of friendship anyone who would spend time talking to her, no matter how little.

She was, in many ways, quite a remarkable woman. She was attractive, intelligent, helpful at the slightest provocation, sensitive and understanding, yet it was as if all her qualities were turned inside out and prostituted by the hunger that consumed her. She was not alone or friendless by any means, yet I think she knew more of the very nature of loneliness than most people because of her fear of it which possessed her life perhaps with the same intensity, creating the same kind of dialogue, or pitched battle, as Pain did with mine.

Her husband was Italian, but she was not, as I first thought, starved of English contacts, in fact her contacts with the English-speaking population were many and varied, yet they did not satisfy some consuming need in her. I don't know why it was she latched onto me, though it was possibly the fact that on our initial acquaintance I had helped her out. Her Italian was not so bad, far better than mine, yet she had been in great difficulties in the market. It became clear that it was not so much the language that was her problem as this deep-etched longing for a contact, some communication, some unfulfilled consummation that drove her towards other people in the search for this undefined goal. She was compulsively helpful. Perhaps she was longing to be helped herself. But I could not work out what it was that she so much needed, what fulfilment so constantly eluded her.

Her requests for coffee, butter, sugar, were all thinly-veiled excuses for contact and conversation. Yet her talk was by no means all of a confessional nature, it was not so much that she came to unburden her soul of her private thoughts or longings, it was more as if she came bearing something in front of her that she wished to present or defend, and this always preceded her through the door. And so it came about that I experienced the first intimation of her arrival somewhere in the region of my solar plexus, a jangling feeling which I came to recognise with apprehension. There was little chance of escape, for if I went out when this feeling first appeared in me, I would be sure to meet her coming up the stairs. And anyway, as a result of my own battle with Pain, I had a gloomy conception of what destiny meant, and believed that it was my fate to sit passively and wait for what had to be, to allow the form of the day, my day, to be swamped and disintegrated by her arrival, her presence, her installation in my apartment and my consciousness and to sit out the encounter with endurance, watching the beginnings of the shape I wanted the day to take dissolving in her presence.

Afterwards, I would reassemble what pieces I could, but more often than not the attempt was unsuccessful, my plans were scattered, my concentration was blitzed, and the day was anaemic. As the process became more recognisable so did my realisation that something had to be done. I harboured all kinds of fantasies about packing various groceries for her in a box, a third of a packet of tea, quarter of a pound of sugar, two or three tomatoes, filling the box brimfull of minute quantities of useful and necessary items, and presenting them to her at the door, closing it behind me and sailing off down the steps. But I never did. It remained in my imagination, a burgeoning array of groceries, collaborating with this woman's inarticulate longing, to cram the space I had intended to stake out and claim as my own, full of the trivia of existence that I had hoped that a different city and a different country would deliver me from.

Her visits were always accompanied by some request. What was it she wanted, I wondered, apart from the sugar, the coffee, the matches? One morning she came early, just as I had set out my canvas and oils, the coffee was bubbling on the stove, and anticipation was welling in me, the first fruits of the morning, the delicious preparation of energies before the first paint touched the canvas. Then the knock on the door. The morning drained from me as she walked in. She apologised for coming so early, but, strangely, no request was on her lips. Without that there was nothing to initiate conversation. The coffee was ready, so I offered her some. She sat down at the table, her hair pulled back from her face, tied back with a thin strip of scarf, and the curls spilling out around the knot. Her skirt was long and full, her shirt loosely draped, with patterns as delicate and intricate as Persian carpets, dark subtle colours blending into each other and caught in at the waist by her skirt, a blooming shade of geranium red. She was attractive and yet, I realised as I passed her the coffee, quite untouchable. Was this her secret longing, her unfulfilled desire? She sat stiffly, hunched over the table. But I could not so much as touch her lightly on the shoulder, not one reassuring gesture could I give her. I wondered about her life of touch. She had two children, not quite in their teens. Did she miss the cuddles and embraces of her children who were no longer interested in this kind of contact? And her husband, did he give her affection, or was he too involved in his own life and work to notice her except at night, her lean body in its accustomed place in the bed beside him, so that there was no effort to be made to reach her, she was there, physically accessible though maybe as remote in her being from him then, as she seemed to be now, from me? Did he fuck her, or did he make love to her, did he give her affection, or did he merely satisfy the longings of his own flesh that her proximity aroused in him, and once satisfied, turn his back to her in bed? Did he find her as untouchable as I did?

That made it seem like a challenge to me. My apartment consisted of two rooms, the huge, red-tiled living-room cum studio, and the tiny bedroom off it. The stove and the sink were in one corner and there I cooked, here by the low table I ate, and the rest of the room was taken up with easel, canvasses, paints, rags, turpentine and brushes in various stages of usage or decay. It was untidy, but I had come here to escape all varieties of conventional ways of life, and I had determined to live in the way that was most comfortable for me, without having to consider anyone else's prejudices or beliefs or preferences. The way Jack would clear up after me, wash the dishes, wash out my brushes, cook for me sometimes, in his agonising — to me — helpfulness, clear things away when I wanted them left just as they were to provide continuity for me so that the next morning I would not have to begin again, but simply pick up where I had left off, and go on. The way he would wait for me sometimes in bed, wait without complaining, wait for that monstrously deceptive moment when our bodies touched and all the rest seemed so unimportant that I renounced it, every night I renounced my own life, gave it over to this other who cleared up so patiently behind me, waited for me so patiently to give up on my own life, my own desires and activities that seemed — once he had touched me — so senseless and so selfish and so trivial, compared to this. And yet — and this was where my understanding stumbled, and could find no foothold — in the night he turned his back on me. He could not sleep, he said, with his arm around me, my head resting on his chest. He had to turn away from me, after all his patient waiting, after all his efforts, all his silent solicitude. Or was it merely preparation for his own satisfaction I wondered, in the nights when I could not sleep, yet his body lay so close to mine, so close I could just move my fingers to stroke it, and often did, yet there was no response, for he was far away in his own vivid world of dreams.

The point of physical contact was our only meeting-ground. And that ground — for me — was where I surrendered everything that I had worked so hard on during the day, everything I had built up, created, striven to hold together in an orchestration of the soul, guiding, shifting, encouraging and engineering, to create a unity out of the fragmenting splinters the day always threatened to become, the ecstatic entropy of tidied rooms, with nothing out of place, that was my personal antagonist, spirit of the closed fist and the locked door and the desertedness of spotless rooms. I worked with a compulsiveness I had no time to analyse for at some wordless level of urgency I knew in some place of my being that I was working to create myself, the forces of dissolution could destroy me and continually, I was working to resurrect myself. And in the night, in that first touch, my efforts melted into a pool of unconstructed being, and all I ever wanted was to be one with this wordless, endless flow, all breath, all flesh, all longing made simple and immense and all-encompassing and one, just with this touch.

But Pain took up its residence with us. Pain in the night, with this wall of back beside me. Pain in the morning which had to be delivered to the work of becoming myself again, this lonely canvas-coverer, this lonely artistry of mirror-making in any image that I chose, for any image would be better than the sea or source of being that reflected everything without differentiation, without choice or form. I had to wrest identity from the flood of morning. I chose my morning mirrors without precision or forethought, bearing only desperation with me from the untuned, chaotic wealth of night.

And it was curious the way it happened sometimes, or so I thought at first, but as it became more frequent, there seemed to be something more to it than mere coincidence the way that sometimes in the morning, just as I had located the beginnings of a shape I could turn the morning into, Jack would turn to me again and in one touch, obliterate the delicate possibilities I had discovered or selected and I was swimming in the soundless water-world of him, his subtle pressure making me abandon the faint hold I had of a picture separate in any way from him, as easily as a wave washes over sand.

So did he pervade my body and my being with the faintest touch. Had the choice been mine, I always would have chosen this ocean of unending being his touch turned me into. But the presence of Pain, in time not diminishing but increasing, forced me to reformulate my primitive conceptions.

Pain lingered through the day, an insistent and determined presence. I struggled to work, while Jack cleared up around me, infinitely helpful, comforting and patient. Then at night, Pain cleared like mist, but its absence was brief and its reappearance came to be so predictable that I lost trust until Pain finally infiltrated even our most intimate embraces. At some point after that, I left. And came to this Italian town that I only knew from books and pictures and the memories of friends. I excised most of my memories of Jack. I figured it would be easier in this unknown place, with so many new impressions to hold my interest and prevent my mind slipping back over Pain's threshold into his far-flung, well-entrenched domain, with roots like arthritic fingers, branches with their backs turned to the sun, and foliage like evanescences of subterranean mist, limp and humid, always sticky to the touch, never crisp or dry, never asserting individual existence but always clinging to the form or taste of whatever last touched it, rubbing its identity off on something else, eradicating singularity, asserting a creeping communality, damp-fingered tendrils to bind you to its world of undifferentiated, undirected blind desire.

And now this woman had appeared, like one of Pain's couriers, moving always within this sticky, loaded world, forever brushing against foliage, pursuing a goal that she could not see clearly, but could only grope her way towards. To sit down and tell her my most recent life history would never have freed her. She needed to be reached in a place where the rest of her life was passing her by. This I saw as her continual hunger. And she had also brought back the memories of Jack and made me wonder, for the first time, if Jack had been more of a symbol for me than a person, more a manifestation of something unconscious in me than another being who I could relate to which perhaps was why, for all that we had lived together, his essence had been so hard to capture, to define, and all our efforts to become each other and to reach each other had driven us more deeply into Pain's kingdom, the mirror-world where all is familiar and yet subtly altered, where nothing is as it seems and where each embrace is thrown back on itself and the greater the longing for contact, the more swiftly will the embrace evaporate in the mists and shades of Pain's deceptive kingdom. This thought gave me a clue. Had it been a part of myself I had been trying to embrace, to unite with, when I was with Jack? Had I been trying to grasp a reflection of myself which was why it had remained so elusive? Was that the point at which you enter Pain's gate?

As I said, I saw it as a challenge. I had not been drawn to this woman in the simple unbounded way I had been drawn to Jack. Something in her repelled me, yet with the eye of distance I saw her hunger settling like a day in summer with no clouds on the horizon, clear of encumbrance or any desire to change. I was not drawn to her, yet something drew her to me and its lack of fulfilment was tugging the bright threads out of my days, divesting them of wholeness, bleaching them of life.

I put my arm around her shoulder, fascinated by the mixture of feelings this aroused in me, a repulsion that was countered by my impersonal determination. A spark shot through me like a connected circuit, and she pulled me to her with a voltage of desire that would have sent any more highly developed sense for survival than mine hurtling to the other side of the room. But I have a high capacity for Pain and its attendant dangers and I have this curious desire to skirt the very boundaries of Death and know of it as much as I can learn without losing a connecting thread with Life, so I let the charge flood through me and held onto her, in the electric storm of her embraces. But I had to do something too, to prevent being completely detonated by her passion, which was none of mine, and since I could not move out of this situation, I moved further in, and drew my hand across her breast and then came the thought that dissolved my will, for I wondered, in that moment, if this was how Jack felt when he touched my body and the thought of him, the memory of him turned my determination into a road that ended with no goal or meaning, just a tailing out into a country filled with liquid sand, submerging purpose, drowning the tracery of meaning and any sound or vision that might give structure to intent. Awash in sand, my heart slumped, and the doorbell rang.

I had only met her husband once before when I ran into them both across the street and was introduced, but my effusive welcome that morning was real enough. I showed him the way into my studio, and locked myself in the bathroom. At first their voices were very low, then they were raised, and the tempo quickened. Then a prolonged silence. I decided it was time they continued their dialogue, or lack of it, elsewhere, and emerged from the bathroom, giving plenty of noisy warning before I did so, but there was still an awkward silence when I went into the studio. Eventually her husband stood up and apologised for disturbing me. She sat still, hunched over the table.

It was too much for me. I started washing out some brushes that were already perfectly clean, took down from the easel the canvas that I had just set up that morning, put on my paint-smeared shirt I used for working in and her husband became more restless, his eyes flickering around the studio as if he had only just noticed his surroundings. Then he asked me about the paints I used and the subjects I chose, polite questions to fill in the space between us, while she said nothing, not looking at him or the canvasses, but at me, and I avoided her eyes, frenziedly tidying up and arranging, wiping and drying, replying to her husband's questions and wondering what I would do when I could create no more preparatory tasks and the words ran out and there was nothing between me and the empty canvas apart from these two people.

"I think perhaps we should go and let your friend get on with her work," her husband said.

Some conventional gesture almost fell out of my mouth before I had time to turn my head and look at them, my mouth still open. And as I looked at them, she stood up uncertainly and when I saw them standing together I could see that nothing had changed and any idea of mine that anything I could do would make any radical alteration in their lives was absurd. The only change that had been effected was in me because I knew, as looked at them, that I would have to leave.

That evening, as I was packing my things, Pain returned and I welcomed it, because it was no longer all jangled up with memories of what had been, and it felt infinitely more real than this curious existence I had tried to stake out for myself which had turned into a drama of the absurd. Pain then felt like a natural reminder that I was alive, that there was nothing to be renounced except the past and that the future held a burgeoning harvest of possibilities, and that is why I welcomed it, like some old friend turning up to restore to you some mislaid, dislocated part of yourself.

Early the next morning, the sky was streaked with colours and the outlines of the buildings were stretched across it like some final canvas that the night had silently prepared and had finally displayed in the bright face of the morning. I sent Jack a postcard telling him I was on my way back home, and walked through the narrow cobbled streets, canvasses under one arm and suitcase in the other.

THE FOOD PARCEL

Sheena Blackhall

Jean Mathers liked to visit her Uncle John. Every family has its black sheep, and Uncle John was as black an old ram as anyone could wish for — his skeleton did not rattle in the cupboard of kinship — it rumbled like Vesuvius. He lived quite on the other side of town, where paint peeled off anonymous doors, and there wasn't a cranny that wasn't a garbage accumulator.

Her father disliked driving through that quarter of the city — on the rare occasions when he did so, his fists tightened perceptibly on the wheel, and he sneaked anxious looks down crumbling alleyways, as if expecting the full force of a vandals' vendetta to single him out for destruction. He rarely mentioned Uncle John, and when he did, it was with a sigh, as if discussing an Angel fallen from grace.

Uncle John, on the other hand, was only too proud of the ties of kindred. He never missed a funeral, turning up faithfully with the hearse, smiling winsomely at the rows of tut-tutting fur coats and mothballed bowlers sitting in censorious respectability around him.

"Anither ane awa," Uncle John would say, with genuine regret. "Ah weel — he/she had a guid innins."

Furtively, over her hymn book, Jean would examine him with a delicious shudder of disapproval. He always reminded her of Al Capone. His fashion sense had stopped, like a broken clock, in the thirties, and he wore gangster-style pinstripe suits of nigger brown, set off by grimy shirts, his long black hair curled over the collar as lank and greasy as a mechanic's work rag. What had been a handsome mouth had deteriorated into a nightmare of broken stumps and offensive gums, but it was inevitably set in a smile.

His children were a Fagin's litter. They were never free of trouble — a criminal element, from a criminal area, engaging in petty crime as happily as other children seek out conkers or collect eggs. Except that their conkers were lead pipes, and their eggs the confectionery kind, courtesy of Woolworth's.

She asked one of them, once, if fear of discovery did not deter them. "We jist greet, an' promise nae tae dae it again. Greetin's a gran' wye tae get ye aff."

Sometimes the phone would ring, and her father would mutter darkly into the mouthpiece, "It's on page eight o' the papers — three paragraphs, nae less! He should think black burnin' shame on himsel, bringin' his bairns up tae that."

For of course, crime never paid — the cousins were always caught — were eternally awaiting Her Majesty's pleasure, "pending background reports". They were so handsome, too, in a gypsy way, but with a frightening catalogue of sins filed against them. The eldest boy had knifed a rival in a jealous row over a girlfriend; his sister, less flamboyant, had been charged with causing various affrays of a trivial and distressing nature, all the result of a fiery temper, unbridled. But mostly the dreary paragraphs in the papers referred to smalltime thieving, at which they were exceedingly active, but very inept.

One day, word came of a different calibre of misery. Uncle John's wife, Aggie, had left him — run off with one of her son's pals. Jean expected to hear the usual diatribe of disapproval, but quite the reverse. Everyone thought it would be the making of him. Auntie Aggie had never been a favourite with Jean's folk. ... She wore too tight sweaters, heavy mascara, and her husky voice spoke of lurid nights and too many full-strength Capstan cigarettes. She invariably smelt like a female reservoir of John Begg whisky. Yet Jean could imagine her in her courting days, looking like a sultry doll, before child-bearing and poverty had made a cosmetic ruin out of her.

"Naething o' the kin'," snapped Mrs Mathers, shattering the little illusion. "Aggie wis aye a trollop. She picked yer Uncle John up at a bus stop ae nicht. She's bin the damnation o' the puir man — he's better aff withoot her." The family rallied round its skeleton, albeit reluctantly. A food parcel arrived from the country — a pink, trussed hen, goosepimpled, stark, and headless, laid in the depths of a cardboard box, jostled by turnips and other culinary delights. He would not be allowed to starve at any rate.

There remained the vexed matter of who should deliver it, and the

THE FOOD PARCEL

lot fell upon the Mathers family. The visit was made at night,
deliberately brief. They drove through the sparkling lights of the city,
an aurora borealis of neon, past acres of granite gentility, which
gradually gave way to danker, darker houses, seedy patchworks of
concrete and corrugated iron. At last, below on the right, like a black
pariah, lay the squalor of homes that was her uncle's ghetto abode,
respository of the town's unwanted citizens.

The warm putt-putt of the engine died as the ignition key was
switched off. Her father's fingers drummed nervously on the
steering wheel.

"Up ye go wi' the parcel, lassie, an' be quick aboot it. An' gie ma
regards tae yer uncle." This last was said with no great enthusiasm.

John stayed at the top of a crumbling stone stairway, an eyrie
ringed by spittle and dog excretia — the very walls of the lobby were
smeared with filth. As she walked up the gloomy stairs, she felt a
surge of compassion for her uncle — his pathetic pride in his family
— his struggle to bring them up decently, and not one of them worth
a tinker's cuss. At the top step she halted, and struck a match. It
sputtered and went out, but a second one held the flame. She held it
high, peering at the door. It was bare of everything, except a broken
handle, and four names, scrawled in illiterate handwriting; she could
just make out "Mathers" underneath. She knocked imperiously, and
waited. A squinting, grey-haired woman, balding and red-faced,
answered the door. Giving her no time to protest, Jean shoved past
bearing the parcel into the parlour. Uncle John was at his evening
meal — a slimy collation of chips, spread over an old magazine. The
other occupants of the room, all strange to her, took note of her well-
cut clothes and clean appearance, and went on the offensive,
assuming her to be an official of some description and therefore a
threat. The girl experienced a moment of fear, till her uncle's familiar
nasal twang set them at ease.

"Staun' back — yon's Davie's lassie — an' wi' a wee parcel for her
Uncle John!" There were tears of gratitude in his eyes. "Yon's
handsome o' them — richt handsome. Aye — we aye stuck
thegither, the Mathers. Bluid's thicker nor watter. They niver forget
their wee Johnny."

Jean smiled, absentmindedly looking down to the street below.
The car engine had started up again. The visit was over.

FOR BETTER OR ELSE

Ellen McMillan

The punch, when it came, lifted her off the floor and sent her reeling like a blind man, onto the settee and sent her scuttling along the floor looking in vain for shelter. With a deafening scream he tore at her clothing, the sound implying he was the victim. This had surprised her. She was silent, he was screaming. His face was not the face of the man she had married. With each kick he had delivered, he had facial spasms as though he too suffered with each blow he gave. Her head was covered over, her arms provided protection and she had over the years learned not to plead. To plead would be almost fatal. The frenzy went on much longer when she pleaded. She had teeth in her mouth and from the soft, warm spongy feeling she knew some were loose. As the foot came nearer she choked on a piece of tooth and the impact, when it came, knocked the tooth back, and probably saved her some serious damage. Fortunately the children were asleep and heard only the silent chatter as the ambulance men consoled her, and neighbours promised to look after the children. They shook their heads consolingly at her husband, who sat, poor soul, with his head in his hands, to play with, as her gran used to say, when she mock threatened them as children. It was funny violence, it made you think the strangest things. Before the black eye she had wondered what Miss Wilkinson, wee Danny's teacher, would think, because strangely enough, nobody ever came right out and asked, but Miss Wilkinson's look said more than a thousand words. For the sake of the children can't you leave him, her eyes would say, but her lips remained still. But when it came to it, what did Miss Wilkinson know about it, anyway? She sometimes wished she had stayed a Miss.

Everyone looked alarmed, she wanted to tell them not to worry but her mouth wouldn't work. Even the children looked alarmed and they were used to this. She wanted to scream at their wee vulnerable faces, he's finished, so don't worry, it won't happen for a long time, but wouldn't it, each time was getting shorter, and each more frenzied. She looked at her husband as they took her away and she wondered how this had happened. The eyes were brimming with tears and genuine shame, his hands shook as did his head in real disbelief. Shoulders hunched completed the picture, a truly pathetic creature. She laughed into herself, she'd had her hair cut, thinking he couldn't grab it when he went "funny", instead he'd grabbed her clothing or anything else to hand. Before she'd blamed her long hair for making her easier to pull around. Avoid the trigger situations people said, and you look for things to blame, find faults in yourself — even invent some. She switched off the TV tonight to plug in the iron. He looked at her but said nothing. Then he stewed. The *Daily Record* was mauled and finally cast aside, before she switched on the set again. The ironing lay in piles on the table which meant he had to rest his feet on the carpet instead of on the table. The socket in the kitchen was broken, or she would have used that instead. When she'd lifted the ironing she volunteered to make a cup of tea. He didn't want one. She made one for herself. He glared at her. The children had been laughing in the bedroom, but a roar from their dad soon shut them up. That was the way he saw it. They were his sons when he spoke to friends about them, but when they misbehaved they were her weans. She watched TV while he watched her. An excuse was all he wanted, and he could vent his anger, she gave him one.

She fidgeted. "Can you not sit at peace?" he'd roared at her, but she was tired and told him so. "Away to bed then," he'd growled and waited. She said nothing, and he took it as an insult. "So you won't even answer now, who the hell do you think you are madam?" She looked at him appealingly but her eyes were tired. "Don't you look at me like that," he shouted. "Your face has been tripping you all night." Standing up she had picked up her cup and walked away towards the kitchen. He sprang from the chair and caught her shoulder which knocked the cup from her hand and she yelled. He rose to the occasion and gave her something to yell for. Those were his very words. "I'll give you something to yell for, you greetin'faced bitch." But she hadn't yelled after that, he had done all the yelling, groaning and any other thing you cared to mention, she had simply

— not died. Like a dog she had whimpered, like a cat she had curled up and like a snake she had wriggled away. But she couldn't avoid the trigger situation. The phone rang and he had stopped. As though caught in some indecent act, he looked over his shoulder and she felt the pain and humiliation. The doorbell rang and suddenly the room was filled with sound but she was full of silence.

When they carried her down the hall she saw the dirt on the lampshade and the wallpaper peeling. Pinky and Perky were speaking over their police radio and they were matter of fact. You'll be OK their eyes said, we've seen worse than you, and they still go back to them. The front door lay open and in the close stood more neighbours who couldn't find a real reason to enter the house without seeming too nosey. She had only one shoe on and she could feel the crusty blood up her nose. By the look on her neighbours' faces she knew they could see it too. It wasn't like this in the movies, even stretcher victims had a tiny stream of blood which ran from their forehead to their brow not up their bloomin' nose. In the ambulance she felt worse as the kind words poured over her, this was worse than anything else. Humanitarianism could destroy the world in a day. Why couldn't he just look at her accusingly as everyone else did. The soft eyes bathed in sympathy and the hand which stroked her brow turned her resolve to jelly and she wept, not quiet sobs, but great roaring, sloppy, breathless ones.

She knew the housework would be done, it was always done when she was taken to hospital, it was, she supposed, a form of making amends. The children would be looked after by neighbours but even if they were not he would look after them. His family would surround him and there would be plenty for the neighbours to talk about for a time. A short-stay patient she would be. A patching-up job. People like her were looked upon as their own worst enemy, she supposed she was in a way. Money provided a form of security and she had none — she never had money, only the housekeeping and often she was deprived of that. It was true that there were places for battered women now, but how could children be expected to form a stable character in such an unstable environment. They didn't always fight anyway, and despite everything she still felt for him, she didn't love him but she felt his anguish. The crisis he like most men suffered from was not the mid-life crisis, but just a life crisis. They couldn't cope with the pressure of being at any time, what they didn't want to be. Identity crisis, they suffered from. The desire to be what the poster said created frustrations they couldn't cope with and the result was they hit out. Some men were better able to curb their violence and divert their unspent energy by channelling it into sport or business or womanising, but an umemployed man or an educated man had to create his own vent. She was very philosophical about it as they wheeled her into the hospital. The young nurses were very kind to her but the young doctor was quite brutally impersonal. He did her a favour by bringing her out of the torrent of self-pity she could have wallowed in.

The police wanted to know if she would press charges against her husband. She wanted to. But she didn't. They left. Only she and the children would suffer, she knew the law and it didn't work for battered wives even in the eighties. Within days she was right as rain, however right rain is. They came to collect her, her husband and boys. The boys looked scrubbed clean and obedient. A taxi waited and they travelled home in style. In the hall she made a mental note to clean the lampshade and keep in mind the peeling wallpaper. She hung her coat on the peg in the hall. At all cost she had to avoid thinking about the last trigger situation, and so she would until the next time, God forbid, think of other things because she didn't know for sure, if when the punch came the next time, it would be the last.

MONSTERS

Susan Campbell

News at Six. Monday.

Blue and grey ghosts flickered around the cubicle, over the multi-coloured carpet of little bodies, up the three white walls, finding an echo in the fourth, made of glass, and in Walter's pallid face, up turned to the enormous screen. He was Switching On To News At Six. All along the opposite block he could see the fluorescent squares blinking and subsiding, and each occupant arranging his family in snuffling ranks around his feet. Walter felt pleasantly exhausted. A large pink rodent climbed into his lap and he petted it with increasing ardour, an infatuated gape rearranging his features as Myreena, his favourite presenter, calmly read out the news. Presently she reached the jokey final item, and Walter, who liked this bit, began to concentrate on what she was saying.

"A 'Monster' made an appearance today on the roof of a university library," she said, a tiny smirk playing around her lips. "These strange phenomena spring up at rare intervals in and around establishments of education. Luckily our National Guard are ready for anything. Guard Maurice Wirt controlled the monster on sight and is now a Major."

The camera cut to an outside shot of a broad grin and two tiny eyes beaming from beneath a green helmet. Travelling down Maurice's squat crumpled uniform, it lingered for a while on his boot, which was raised uncomfortably onto the shaggy hide, almost causing Maurice to topple over backwards. Then the picture widened out and the full length of the monster became apparent. It had the head of an enormous bird, and several tails. There was no blood but it was evidently very dead. Walter, frog-eyed and at a loss for how to react, was relieved by Myreena, back at the studio, wreathed in smiles.

"Maurice de-monster-ating how it's done there, and that's all till tomorrow, when you'll be — Switching On To News At Six!"

After a few moments Walter began to snicker at Myreena's joke. A Soy-Ad was now screened and Walter rose obediently to make dinner for the youngest of his family, so he could get them off to bed before the pet-rearing programme. He placed the pink rat carefully on the floor, and his heart swelled with love as a tighly packed convoy of fur and feathers gravitated with him towards the kitchen door. "Back," he said quietly, and the pets surged back, hopping and heaving, each to its own place on the floor, looking after Walter with soft adoring eyes.

News at Six. Thursday.

Walter, prevented for the first time from exercising a harnessed team of enormous rabbits in the University grounds, was feeling even more fatigued than usual, having had to rearrange entirely his exercise schedules. The University buildings had been cordoned off and deserted, National Guards had asked to see his number and Opcard and ordered him away. He slumped dispiritedly in the chair, staring up at the news, which consisted this evening of an array of government statistics. Myreena was sitting with two politicians round a table, upon which sat a red fluffy puppy and a large tortoise.

"The number of those engaged in full-time Domestic Responsibility has increased dramatically again," Myreena was saying. Both politicians fondled their pets and the Alliance leader was asked to comment.

"In the bad old days," he said, "our ancestors slaved away at 'Jobs' for seven or eight hours a day, to earn money, to support their teeming children. Microchip technology and population control have produced a Caring Society, just as we promised you it would."

Myreena had on her most pleased eyebrows.

"The remunerative Voluntary Purification Scheme is progressing according to plan," she said. "The means-tested payments for the simple operation are being invested in industry, and Interest rates are high and rising. The marriage rate is still steadily decreasing and the birth rate will continue to fall sharply in large sections of the community. The Social Responsibility Subsidy will be awarded later this month to the most progressive zone. A comment from the Feminist Democrat:

"Wimmin are breaking free from the shackles of their oppressors," boomed the Feminist Democrat. "The archaic notion of the 'Family', incorporating Father, Mother and children, is, for the vast majority a thing of the past. No longer are we slaves to men! Not economically, not emotionally, not sexually . . . At this point the red puppy began to lick the face of the Feminist Democrat, fiercely wagging its whole body. Myreena and the Alliance leader allowed themselves misty smiles, heads on one side, and the steely expression of the Feminist Democrat also melted, as if dissolved by licks. Walter appreciated this spectacle with one eye. The other he was screwing up effortfully, still trying to work out all the hard words in what Myreena had said.

He thought that it boiled down to more money in his next Interesting Cheque, which was his only income apart from Pet Allowance. He began to contemplate new winter coats for the squirrels, and, not for the first time, he felt glad of his free housing. He knew that in other zones there were people who had to pay for their houses, and didn't even get Interesting Cheques because the Op wasn't worth it for them because it was Mean Testicle. He had never quite understood this though Arthur next door had explained it to him. He understood though, that these people had children running amok in their houses, making a mess and being cheeky and dirty. Thinking about these social inequalities made Walter feel better, and when Myreena began to tell the viewers about a man who could play tunes by stuffing his fingers up his nose, he laughed uproariously and the pets snorted and snuffled, wagging tails and perking noses and ears in a bristling concentric wave of sympathy.

News At Six. Friday.

When Walter Switched On, Myreena manifested from the expanding black hole peering from beneath strings of flags which bedecked the studio.

"The Monster Crisis is over!" she pronounced.

Walter was taken aback. He hadn't realised there was a crisis on.

"The National Monster Crisis, which has been terrorising innocent citizens for several days, has been brought under control by the government," continued Myreena.

Walter felt relieved to hear it.

"This footage from around the country shows how the National Guard won the day and prevented the potential collapse of society as we know it."

At this point there was a knock and Arthur-next-door shuffled in, paddling knee-deep through the pets. Walter flapped his hand at him and since there was no other chair, Arthur cleared a space on the carpet and creaked down, elbowing away an ancient dog who tried to lean on him. He held back his struggling curtains of grey hair ar d stared up at the screen.

The sharp-edged, block-graph horizon of a University appeared, dark against a lightening sky. At first it was perfectly quiet and still, then, from one corner, there reared a great bear-head, swivelling on a sinuous neck, and a curved talon gripped the roof edge. Another skyline, at nightfall, thin wafers of light blinked from the facade, the flat roof was swelling and cracking and a humped, many-legged beast raised its crocodile jaws to the pale stars. Again the scene changed and a kind of snake with draggled wings slithered from the top of a fire-escape into a dreary sun, where a shark-headed lizard was already basking uneasily. A platoon of National Guards appeared on the screen, kneeling and taking aim. There was a burst of noise, which startled Walter's pets, and each University appeared again, with a misshapen mound upon it, and an ants' nest of green helmets.

Back at the studio a little furrow had appeared on Myreena's brow.

"I have with me this evening the Minister of Education and the Minister of Technology," she said earnestly, "who will discuss this unprecedented outbreak of vicious monsters."

The Minister of Education was crouching in his seat to avoid being festooned with flags, looking glum. He had an old face like a crumpled pàper bag.

"Well," he said, when Myreena asked him to offer an opinion. "These so-called 'monsters' are, of course, not strictly supposed to exist at all, but since the New Plan, and the modification of Education to Occupational Training, it seems that in the studies and corridors of our Universities they have been quietly, slowly and painfully manifesting themselves, consolidating ... breeding perhaps. However, when you say 'vicious' . . . "

Myreena turned to the Minister of Technology and quickly asked him what he thought. From the floor Arthur grunted with annoyance and unfolded his legs, discomposing a cluster of sleeping kittens. Walter glared.

"My good friend and colleague," he said, "is living in the past. He has not yet come to terms with Reality. May I take this opportunity to remind him yet again of the 'information surplus', of the appalling waste which is our inheritance from the days before Occupational Training; of the insinuating generation in our Universities of ideas and even whole areas of study which will not have a function in society. A phenomenon which is linked directly to the present near-catastrophe."

The Minister of Education opened his mouth but Myreena nodded at the other man to continue.

"Today's students," he said, nodding back, "must be taught only what their systems can usefully and easily cope with, so that these students in turn are useful to the greater system of our society, and nothing is wasted. I'll give you a metaphor," he continued, "a picture to help you understand what all this has to do with monsters. You all have dogs and cats and rabbits. Give a pet too much, or the wrong sort of food, and it will sick it up again. Its system has no use for the food. Now what do you think would happen if you left that sick on the carpet? In a little while you would have a nest of beetles and flies and maggots, gorging themselves on the waste. Think of that on an enormous scale. That is what the monsters are. Parasites — growing fat on the excess leaking from the Universities . . ."

"It's not like that at all," interrupted the Minister of Education from off-camera.

"PARASITES," continued the Minister of Technology loudly. "Sniffing on the poisoned air, skulking round the corridors, building themsleves into monsters on the waste, the effluence. . . ."

Arthur jumped up from the floor and started to shout at the television. He did this from time to time in Walter's cubicle, since he had broken his own screen, and Walter turned up the sound on the handset, unsurprised. He secretly believed that Arthur was senile. Arthur maintained that he'd once been going to study Management but he'd failed the University entrance tests. He'd had to give a man shocks to help him learn a puzzle and Arthur had refused to do it, even though really the puzzle man was only pretending to be shocked. Then he had to say which line was longest with a crowd of other students, who were so blind they all said the same wrong answer. Since Arthur kept on saying something different to everyone else he was finally judged to be inaccessible to learning. He often said silly things, and Walter doubted that he had ever been University material, even if he did know hard words. When Arthur had finished shouting he clutched his back and reseated himself gingerly.

"You know," he said after a while, "he's so smug, isn't he — but there's always the one that gets away. Let's hope so anyway."

Walter decided to let him ramble on to himself.

"I heard a funny thing today," Arthur continued, oblivious, addressing a half-circle of bemused furry faces. "I heard that when they catch them alive, they tame them and keep them up at Government House, like pets, and make use of them in some way. I don't know how. . . ."

Walter stared determinedly at the screen, where Myreena was

telling about a man who'd chopped his head off by mistake, and had the presence of mind to pick it up and take it to a hospital, where it was sewn back on.

"That poor old Minister of Education's heading for Domestic Responsibility," said Arthur. "I think the military will take over the Universities any day now. Then they'll really be obedience schools, more than ever."

The ads came on and Walter gawped covetously at a textured squirrel-coat with lasered seams. Arthur also stared at it for some minutes, then he wished Walter goodnight and picked his way carefully out of the room. Walter pitied him, returning to a bare cubicle without a family to welcome him. He decided that if Arthur got any more miserable he would be neighbourly and report it to the authorities.

News At Six. Monday.

"Rumours to the effect that Monsters are being kept as pets in Government House are totally untrue," said Myreena, looking aggrieved. The Prime Minister appeared on a walkabout, kissing dogs and cats and shaking tiny paws. Then Government House came up on the screen, and the King was seen out walking in the grounds with a synchronised formation of fifty Corgis.

"The Minister of Education has gone into voluntary retirement," continued Myreena. "The new Minister of Occupational Training is Maurice Wirt, an ex-Major, and the department will be transferred from a Civil to a Military responsibility."

"And now something to make you smile . . ."

The room exploded inwards. A glittering rainbow of glass from the window-wall sprayed onto the carpet, the pets and Walter, who turned aghast from the television and flung his arms up to protect his face. The crash cut a space of dead silence, except for the twittering of the television; then all the pets with one voice opened up their throats and screamed, yowled, yelped, squeaked and squawked in a terrified frantic chorus. The room was a solid cube of noise.

The monster thrashed desperately from side to side on the carpet, crushing pets beneath the ridge of its spine, and waving useless limbs in the air. It looked broken all over, though it was not bleeding; the red ooze mixing with the splinters on the floor belonged to the pets. It was there, and partly it was not there. Its edges were blurred. Its reptile tail was flaccid and its wolf-muzzle looked soft, spongy, as if all the teeth were gone. One eye was an empty, spreading socket; the other rolled back into the skull, white with fear.

The panic of the pets built to a crescendo. Walter flattened himself against a wall and turned his head, like a Greek frieze, in wild expectation towards the television. There was an appalled hiatus.

The wail of a siren resolved it, and the cubicle poured full of light. A microphone shrieked from the street and the pets whimpered and fell silent.

"Surrender," boomed a slurred artificial voice.

Walter automatically took a blind step forward, lifting up his hand against the light, and his shadow sprawled hugely up the wall behind him. He realised he was being arrested for hiding a parasite in his cubicle.

"Not you," said the microphone.

Walter stopped, confused and squinting.

"You are advised to surrender. You will be well treated and cared for, provided you co-operate."

Again Walter trotted forward, the spider-shadow springing at his heels.

"NOT YOU!"

Walter swallowed and stood very still.

"A harness will be passed through the window. Allow the occupant to harness you or you will be destroyed."

They were talking to the monster! The monster could understand! Walter gazed down at the animal and saw its good eye look back steadily into his face like an old old friend. The missing eye meanwhile, made perforce a dreadful wink. Walter felt something like a roar gathering in his chest, but when it came, it was only a sniffle, and when he was ordered to tie up the harness he obeyed, choking only a little and wiping his nose. He turned, heartsick, from the finished deed, only to crash into Arthur, stamping full tilt over the broken glass and cowering pets. From where he landed on the floor, Walter was only dimly aware of Arthur tugging at the haltered beast and shouting. Then they took him away, and with him the animal, and Walter was left alone. He sat on the carpet and stared out of his broken window until the sky began to brighten. Towards daybreak he stood up and began slowly to pick the pieces of glass off the carpet. He didn't want any of his pets to prick their paws.

* * *

News at Six. Two months later. Monday.

When the new neighbour arrived, he had to Switch On To News At Six with Walter because Arthur had done something funny to the screen next door and it couldn't be fixed in a hurry. The neighbour's name was Brian, and he had a big family, so they watched with pets

two-deep around their feet. Myreena was interviewing a General.
"General Wellbeing has recently enjoyed a meteoric rise to success
in the Military," she said. "He is in the studio today to tell us about
the breakthrough, for which he is responsible, which will make this
country great once more." The General said nothing. He was sitting
oddly hunched up, in an ill-fitting uniform bedecked with medals.
He did not look at the camera and his oversized military cap threw
his face into shadow beneath the studio lights. The camera swerved
from him to the Minister of Technology, who was sitting beside him
looking pleased with himself. Realising he was on screen, he began
to speak:
"The General's idea constitutes a huge stride forward in
humanitarianism," he said. "He has invented a wholly new type of
nerve gas, the effect of which is painlessly to make the recipient
accessible to learning. Trouble spots all over the globe can now be
subdued without indiscriminate loss of life! All prejudice and hatred
can be done away with!"
Myreena looked impressed and asked the General to explain the
principle of the new gas. The General kept his head down and
answered in a curious gasping yelp, swallowing his words:
"The gas blocks a certain neural transmitter at the synaptic button,
differentially in certain brain cells only, and not throughout the
nervous system, as is the case with conventional nerve gas. The
amygdala is essentially deactivated, blocking rage and aggression
responses. There are possible side effects of loss of memory and loss
of sexual activity."
When would the General's plan be implemented, asked Myreena
quickly.
"The proliferation of enemy arms gives much cause for concern,"
said the General awkwardly. "World annihilation must be avoided.
As we speak the gas is being released over selected population
centres in the Other Half."
As he said this, he looked at the camera for the first time. Walter
stared at the familiar wolf-like jaws and the eye-patched wink. The
beast's good eye was dulled with defeat. Walter gave a small shriek
and a rabbit fell off his lap.
"Plug ugly, isn't he?" said Brian. "One of them foreigners I'll bet.
Sounds like he knows a thing or two, mind."
Walter reached for the handset and switched channels.
"What's the matter with you?" said Brian. "Not watching News At
Six? That's a bit off."
Walter did not reply. He recovered his rabbit from the floor and
began to stroke it mechanically, gazing up at the screen, although it

109

showed only the test card of the dog and bone. After a while he switched back to News at Six, just in time to be informed that the Prime Minister's donkey had given birth to triplets.

THE INCIDENT AT BAYONNE

Jane Morris

We lived in swimsuits and day followed innocent day. It has all strained through my sieve-like memory with hardly a lump; there was no friction to grip the imagination. Even my birthday could not possibly stand out. When we woke that morning Thomas asked, "What would you like to do?" and I said, "The same. It suits me perfectly." Yet there are one or two points that stick out of that smooth, contented reminiscence. I'd like to forget them but I can't, like sore thumbs that you have to go on using. And so I keep on chewing over in my memory the hedgehogs, the horror at Bayonne Station, and the hotel in Bordeaux.

I'd been a strict vegetarian for nearly three years when we went on that holiday, but it was self-catering, so that was OK. Neither of us drive, and as I walked the daily mile to the fruit-market I agonised over the squashed hedgehogs on the road and I hated the Volkswagens and Citroens that had reduced the fat, ambling things to a stain of guts. I wondered if it hurt very much to be killed like that and I wondered if the car-drivers could feel it when they ran over a small animal. But to tell the truth, both of us agonised about the prospect of returning, Thomas to his laboratory, me to the hospital, home to hard work and weather both.

"The two days of travelling might be fun," I said.

"I'll be satisfied if they pass without incident," said Thomas.

Our bus threaded through the pine-forests of the Landes as far as Bayonne. As it crossed the river we glimpsed the twin spires of a medieval cathedral down cobbled streets. I said, "What a shame there isn't time to look round!"

Bayonne station has the charm of delicate, wrought-iron calligraphy executed with repeated flourishes and arcs on fine graph-paper. They haven't installed the orange plastic seats that ruin the same elegance at Bordeaux. The passengers, less international than in larger towns, underline the Frenchness of its allure, a particularly French flavour that began to fade in the fifties. We savoured it.

"If I wasn't French in my last incarnation, I hope I shall be in the next." I grinned, to show I didn't really mean that. But nearly. I really loved the dishevelled strictness of that old French style, the formality of old men in berets rather than bowlers, children in "short" trousers down to their knees and small boots rather than shoes, some of them wearing their school overalls. I admired the elegance of middle-aged ladies in dark dresses and high heels but no stockings in the heat. The people talked quietly in small groups around their leather luggage under the shade of the station canopy. Two teenage girls shared a vanilla-scented cigarette. A porter crossed the line with a bicycle under each arm. A fashionable lady emergéd from the subway with two Pekinese on long leads. No one took any notice of anyone else, it seemed.

Thomas remarked, "A lady has collapsed."

"Where?"

He pointed.

"Look after this."

I dropped my rucksack and ran as fast as I could. The same reflex that sprinted me to the unconscious woman then made me tell the bystanders, "Je suis médicin." "Médicin indeed?" thought my real self. More precisely, I am a Scottish psychiatrist, and a trainee at that.

I knelt beside the old woman where she lay on the ground. She was a large, comfortable shape, even unconscious. Her nylon carrier bag had been folded to cushion her head. A trickle of blood ran from her right hand where she had grazed it, falling. She was grey-faced. A middle-aged man squatted on the other side of her body, holding her hand and pleading, "Maman!" In his other arm he had a child of two or three who buried her head in his pullover.

I pushed the woman onto her side in case she might vomit, but she did not. I hooked a finger into her mouth for anything removable, but any false teeth were wired to the rest. I pulled her back over and felt for a carotid pulse. Something was beating fast and lightly — perhaps my own finger. I gave her one quick thump on the sternum. The son flinched, but she did not respond. I felt again for the carotid, then timed my own pulse. Mine was slower, though not much. She breathed then, with a sigh.

"Madame!" I shouted into her ear.

"Maman," murmured the son, in apology.

At that point, the reflex which had activated me so far came to an end and I was on my own again with an unconscious woman at the centre of a small crowd. Dumb stares all round.

"Thomas!" I called, "have they sent for an ambulance?"

One of the gaping crowd was dressed up like a station-master in a farce, in braided coat, cylindrical cap and carrying a satchel. He informed me, in French so formal it sounded spiteful, that indeed an ambulance had been called, urgently. "Elle est morte?" He made the question reproachful.

"Pas encore," I told him.

I cross-examined the son, and his little girl lifted her head to stare at me. Was the old lady hypersensitive, diabetic, epileptic? No. Taking any medication? None. Had she been ill recently? Never in her life. She was a healthy eighty-five-year-old woman who had been visiting her family and was now returning to her sister in Bordeaux. She was his mother, she could not possibly die. His voice shook. I glanced at the child but she refused to meet my eyes and buried her head again. She looked remarkably like her grandmother.

By now the emergency team had arrived. Greek gods in pure white tunics, not at all like our own crumpled casualty officers, came flying across the station, crossing the lines directly, not using the subway. The station-master presented himself for interrogation, the woman's son let himself be led away, and death was certified over the hump of clothes on the platform. I was rendered superfluous in time to notice Thomas lifting up the two rucksacks in great agitation, and the train pulling out. "Jump! Jump!" he cried, but French railway carriages have high steps and I was frightened to leap onto the moving train. The station-master watched us. There was nothing he could do to hold the train, he said, there was another in four hours.

"Four hours!" said Thomas. "Tell him you're a doctor and you've been trying to help the woman. You were the only one with any idea what to do, then this is how they treat you." He didn't need to translate his frustration to the expressionless official, and turned away, quietly cursing. The Bordeaux train was still visible in the distance. I argued with the man again. He said no, there was nothing for it but to wait, madame, and walked away, to end the dispute. I ran after Thomas. "At least we can telephone Bordeaux and reserve a hotel room," I said, and did so, feeling rather smug that I could handle a French call-box.

We spent our four-hour wait visiting the town and its cathedral. We were both silent after we'd asked the way across the river. I couldn't stop thinking about the death, though I had no idea what to think — my attitude I mean. Old women die all the time in hospitals. Why is it so terrible when it happens in public? Thomas was ashen and I realised he'd never seen a dead body before. I remembered those early days when a human corpse was a fearful thing to me too. No wonder he looked grim, I thought, and squeezed his hand, but he couldn't manage a smile.

We toured the cathedral. One or two women were actually praying in there and I toyed with the idea of lighting a candle for the dead woman, but rejected it. Then those squashed hedgehogs came into my mind. I rejected them even more firmly. No point getting sentimental about death.

On the way back to the station we saw an old woman, a skeleton in rags, delving in the garbage for scraps. A bunch of well-dressed teenagers with expensive books and bikes had stopped on their way from school to jeer at her. We watched them watch her fury. Then we walked on. This old woman would have to fend for herself.

The pretty station, when we reached it, was cool and bland. Butter wouldn't melt in its mouth. Old gentlemen in berets and light jackets, children in knee shorts, their elegant high-heeled mothers, all stood beside their leather luggage as if nothing had happened, the perfect alibis. I hated them all.

The train took its time. I rested my head on Thomas's shoulder and dozed.

At the hotel, it took me longer to fall asleep than I'd expected, because of the hard, cylindrical bolster fixed under the bottom sheet and tied down both ends. I knew we'd have stiff necks in the morning. I rarely wake in the night but this was an exception. About two o'clock the bar below us closed and the roistering continued below our window. Doors slammed, glasses smashed. Someone vomited audibly in the lavatory downstairs, feet creaked up the stairs, a nose was blown forcibly in the room next door, someone searched for a particular radio station, flushed a bidet. When all that stopped a late mosquito came buzzing to and fro across my face and drove me frantic. I managed to kill it. Then I saw I had woken Thomas.

"No you didn't," he said, "I wasn't asleep."

"Did the mosquito wake you too?"

"I haven't slept at all."

His face was wet. He buried it in my neck.

"All the time we were at Bayonne and you thought I was upset, I was just furiously angry we'd missed the train. I didn't want to help, I just stood and stared like all the other dummies. None of us knows

how to help each other any more. I'm so sorry."
 I stroked his hot back and stared at the dark wall beyond, grimly.

THE LETTER

Iris Doyle

You'll wonder why I'm writing this and not telling you face to face
or even rushing to the phone and sending frantic words down the
line. You'd like that wouldn't you? You'd like to hear my frantic voice
and hear me thundering at your door pleading to be let in like some
demented cat after a rainstorm. It would suit your sense of drama.
Tough.

Have you got the gist that this is a very angry woman speaking to
you through these words? I hope so. I hope you have a sense of
words seething on pristine paper, words that want to reach out and
do you great harm, words that want to lurch at your throat and tear
out your jugular. Yes. That would do quite nicely.

And yet I have this vision of you flicking through all this with
bored disregard, the lips smiling benignly as you think it is only, after
all, rubbish. That would be *so you*. You dismissing what doesn't suit.
God, I wish I could spit the words on this page into your eye.

You'll be chuckling now, seeing me as the true hysteric you always
told me I was. God that's a laugh, *me* hysterical? Was it not you that
used to . . . no, I won't go into all that, it's quite irrelevant now. But I
can imagine you. And after your derision will come your sorrow.
What, you will ask yourself, have I done to deserve all this? You will
search and search deep into your soul (you *were* always telling me
you thought with your *soul*), and you will ponder why you are so
accursed and baited. Ponder no more, I'm about to lay it on the line.
Ready?

It has come to my attention that you have been seeing Rachael. Did

I say 'seeing' Rachael? See, you've even got *me* deluding *me* now! But
no need to enter into graphics, I'll take it that when I refer to you
'seeing' Rachael you'll know that I know just to what extent you have
indeed viewed herself. My opinion of Rachael I shan't bore you with,
I'll let that little card land flatly on her own sweet self, but I did think
that it might be nice to let go of what I think of you.

But first I must try and think for myself, that's the first thing. I have
listened to you and thought and said what you told me to think and
say for so long that I must be careful here and make sure I use *my*
words and not *yours*. So how shall I put it? Where are the words? See
how befuddled I am? We keep telling each other, all us collective
women, not to fall into this trap and yet here I am, just like a fool, in
the very trap I steered others clear of. That I should find myself so
brings great sorrow but when we lay the blame for everything at your
two-faced feet, we'll put that one there as well for surely that's where
it belongs.

Was I blameless? You'll be asking yourself that very same question
about me. Go ahead. Ask yourself. I can even predict your answer
. . . that you were not wholly responsible, if responsible at *all*. But
that's OK. You go ahead and lie to yourself. I don't care. What's it to
me if you've to run battering at some priest's door one night near the
end of your sweet life looking for absolution as you confess that
you've lied, not only to the general public, but even to yourself for all
your rotten life? But don't worry, the priest should be able to take it
even if you can't, they train them to, they're used to dealing with
losers like you all down the line of their contained lives. Or have you
given up your Catholicism as well as me? God, that would be a lark.
I remember in your poetic phase how you'd sought conversion like a
gold panner up at the Yukon. Eager you were, gesticulating and
sublimating all over the place. All true poets turned on the road to
Rome at some point, you said. Trouble was, you turned without the
poetry. Oh, I know, I know. I'll admit it now, I *lied* when I said I liked
your poetry. There, it's out. But what did you want of me? And yes,
I lied too the time I said I might have a bash at Catholicism myself. I
might as well tell you. But really. Did you really think you were
serious? I didn't. You didn't fool me for one bit. A set of rosary beads
and a missal don't really make a pope now do they? It was only yet
another of your romantic dreams. And it got out of hand, it really
did. Did you really think that post-conversion you and I would stand
at some altar pledging our troths and then walk off into a sunlight
dappled with numerous children to be brought up in the faith?
Because I didn't, I didn't really think it for one minute. You thought
all women sought such romance didn't you? You really thought that.

And me being a woman you presumed that I would be in there with the rest just begging for a dream. God, don't make me laugh. But it does show what I mean. You only heard me say what you wanted to hear. You heard me speak *your* words to you, not my ones. Not ever my words. But you're hearing them now.

And how, you will ask in a confused way, did I get to even *know* about Rachael? That was easy. Rachael told me about Rachael. Oh, I forgot, she hasn't told you she's told me yet has she? That's cute. It puts a new slant on that one about the aggrieved always being the last to know doesn't it? Yes. The other night over a first cup of coffee she told me she had been seeing you. That's nice, I thought, and me being a big person didn't think anything of it. So she was seeing you. So what? How nice, I thought. How very *now* and *today* and my weren't we all very grown up? How stupid. By the second cup of coffee I knew that 'seeing' was a misnomer. Well, well, well, I thought. Traitoring. Who would have thought it? Who would have thought it of you? Who would even have considered it of Rachael? But there we were, us two grown-ups chatting about you as though you were the recent book. Does that shock you? Did you not think that women got down to the nitty gritty, and I mean gritty, of things? Well, keep reading kid, you'll learn more.

I didn't know that you'd been suffering from impotence. Didn't see any signs of it but there we are. I must be stupid. Rachael told me how she helped you out. It was very big of her. Very big of her indeed. She also told me that you wanted it to be a little secret between yourselves. That was cosy. But she told me all about you and your whimpering and how low you were about your little spot of impotence and how she had sorted all that out now so that was fine and how she and I could keep what she had told me as *our* little· secret.

So there we have it, all these little secrets are out of the bag now. You didn't think that Rachael would traitor on you after traitoring on me did you? Eh? Bet that comes as a jolt. But it's like I always said, you should have listened to *me*, I could have told you Rachael wasn't the secretive type at all. But too late.

And what a low-down line. Impotence. It's quite original, I'll give you that and you appear to play the part well according to Rachael's account of the event, but *really*, what a trick to use. And to think that you once said in a mad alcoholic fit that you were giving it all up because of your beliefs! Huh, you give up something that was *yours*? That's a laugh. The only thing you give up on are the people you own. And you did own me, make no mistake about that. Heart, body and soul I was yours. Not right for a woman of my time, not right at all but there we have it. Collectively we women are strong as steel rivets, solitary we're just like we always were, God help us.

But to *think* that you and Rachael. Well, well, well. Does it make you cringe? Does it make you feel like a snail? Not because, I may add, of you and Rachael, but because I've found out about you and Rachael. I mean, I can't see you having qualms about the event itself but maybe being found out disturbs you? You wouldn't like that. You don't like your calm being disturbed.

Do you remember that time I was nearly pregnant? Well, not *nearly* pregnant, you can't actually *be* nearly pregnant, but that time I *thought* I was pregnant. Do you remember? Your calm was disturbed there all right. How you had ranted, I had never seen you rant so and how you had the gall to keep asking me why *I* had done this to *you* I'll never know. And then the panic, my, how you panicked. Before I knew where I was you were on the one hand working out what a mortgage would cost as you wanted a house with a nursery room for *your* baby and on the other you were finding out just how quick I could be 'seen' to and whether a N.H.S. hospital would be prompt enough or would you have to get me to go private and if so what would it cost because you had, after all, been planning on buying those new skis. God, when I write it all down it looks even more ridiculous than it was, but there we have it, such were the ways of your world. And then the relief when you found out it had been a false alarm. Don't deny it, I know just how relieved you were. But did you have to make that joke to me, hah-hah, about how you hoped I hadn't been putting you on just to try and force your hand? I didn't like that joke. But do you know what I remember most? You never once asked me what *I* felt, if *I* was relieved. Not once. But then, you never asked me much, you just presumed for the two of us.

Oh, I know that makes me sound ineffectual, it makes me sound so weak and clawing, as though I would do anything, take anything, just so I might have you. I know it makes me sound all of these things. But you know, that's just how it was. That is exactly the way it was with us. I cringe at the thought.

But Rachael was my Waterloo. I draw the line at that. OK, so we weren't *married* or anything so it's not adultery (doesn't that sound so old and quaint in these times?), but wasn't it you who always told me that what we had was *more* than a marriage? Wasn't it you who insisted (apart from when you got silly about your conversion) that you and I were already as *one*? I think it was but even more annoying than that was the fact that I believed you.

Fickle, fickle friend and fickle fate have undone all that now. I believed so much in all you said. I even dyed my hair for you because you like auburn hair. Can you believe that? Me, who doesn't like cosmetics because they test them out on little animals, rushed out to a chemist and bought hair dye and inflicted myself to hours of change. I even started to cook all those 'brown' foods for you and even dallied with the idea of the Communist Party when that mad flight had crept into your brain. And even, God forgive me, I started to clean for you. Yes, I started to clean for you because you didn't like untidiness. I swept and polished and put things away before you called round here because I wanted to please.

And now it has come to this sad state. You and Rachael. Rachael and you. I roll the words round my tongue as though I'm learning a foreign language and I can't get the accents right. It *is* a foreign language. So sod you chum. Sod Rachael. And if I could just get rid of this anger I could cast both of you aside with a flick of the wrist and get on with the rest.

Or maybe I shouldn't feel anger? Maybe I should be full of compassion, sympathy, and understanding? Sod that. I'm angry.

When I think of the things I did for you. I know, I know, I shouldn't think, it never does do any good, but there we have it, I think. I think and think and think and it spins round my head like a whirling dervish and I feel sick.

I think of so many things, things I've done for you, times I cared for you. Do you remember that time I looked after you when you were recovering from your appendicitis operation? I cancelled a trip to London so I could tend to your needs. So what's a trip to London? I'll tell you what it is, it's bloody lovely compared to rushing about your flat tending your needs and then sitting up half the night massaging your back because you can't sleep, that's what it is. I know I didn't mind, not at the time, I did keep telling you that I didn't mind didn't I? But I was a fool, I should have minded very much. But that's the way it goes. C'est la friggin' vie. And I not only mind now. I seethe. I seethe and rage.

Maybe I do you a great kindness that I don't come to your door and merely write all this down because I think I might murder you if I was near you.

But should I even be writing to you? Do you deserve as much as a letter being delivered to your door? Why does some poor postman have to pound up those bloody stairs of yours just so *you* can get mail? See how angry I am? If I had my way no one would even deliver mail to you ever again. That's what I would do. I would make it that life didn't come near you at all and you were left to fester alone. The world would turn from you and there you would be, a lone voice in exile that the world chose to ignore because it was the voice of a rat.

THE LETTER

But I'll let this one last letter be delivered to you and maybe by then the world will be a wiser place and not go near you. My voice might be the last voice you ever hear.

I tell you, come and lift any things here that might belong to you and come quickly because if they're not removed soon they might be little pieces of things thrust into a polythene rubbish bag. Come and remove them and maybe while you're here you might consider removing the lovely Rachael as well or she may end up the same sweet way, thrust up. Oh, I forgot, you like to live *alone*, to have, as you put it, time to *be*, time to *think*. OK. Leave Rachael here then, but come and get your things. Don't, should I be here when you call, even look at me. Don't try to utter one pathetic word in your defence or in apology because I'm not listening. Just come and get your things and be gone. You can't sweep me up in your arms like they do in those books, I'm not dust and your vague masculinity can't overwhelm me, just come and go. And don't give me the crap that you thought you and I were forever, just get the stuff and go, it's taking up room. And don't use the key that you were once welcome to use, knock as though you were a stranger and I'll let you in. And that will be that. I'll be forced to look on you but never mind. It will pass. All things pass. Well look at us, we passed.

Or maybe it's better that we don't look at us? Maybe that's not a good idea at all, who knows what it might lead to? So don't come. Don't come then we can't see us together again and stir old sad memories. It means your stuff will have to stay here taking up room but never mind, better clutter than a broken heart. That's better isn't it? Who needs a broken heart?

Right then, that's settled, I won't see you and you won't see me and everything will be fine. So this is it. Finished. It wasn't terrific, but there we have it. You caused me pain and humiliation but we'll just leave it there.

No, sod it. We won't just leave it there. You know what's going to happen next? I'm coming to see you. Yes, that's it. I'm coming to see you. I will pound up those stairs and save the postman the trouble, I will use a clenched fist and knock at your romany coloured door and you, sweet heart, will open it.

There I will be, standing looking frightful, you'll take a deep breath and that's when I'll plunge the knife that I'm about to fetch from the kitchen cupboard into you.

I hope you die.

THE EVIL PLANETS

Jennifer Russell

The thought-crafts projected telescopic rays down to the planet.

"Two variants of dominant species. One male, one female, clicked Gutkir in thought-speech to his fellow travellers — while simultaneously sending the message more powerfully, but with ease, across the millions of space units between them and their place of origin.

All over their Universe — all that was within sight of the planet Tgir — thought-crafts floated around interesting planets which contained life. The mass launching had taken place one unit of space time earlier, and already all were there. As soon as the blueprint of a thought-craft had been formed in the mind of an idle and imaginative Tgiram, it had come into effective actuality before his eyes. He was now hailed as a genius because, despite the mental powers of his species, most scientific wishful structures crumbled without hundreds of units of space time's concentration on even the simplest — which no Tgiram was inclined towards, having little ambition. His feat had been a pure and spontaneous invention, always the most powerful. The planet had celebrated to the unknown power that they loved, thanking it for this gift of space travel. It was a true miracle, as Tgirams lived perfect lives with their powers of making simple thought forms actual forms, and had no need to spend the units and units of time necessary for scientific, logical progress. Didtrig, the inventor of the fleet of thought-crafts which could travel as fast as sight, had stumbled on the most sophisticated form of space travel ever yet brought about. On the planet Tgir, all Tgirams closed

122

their eyes and flicked mentally from miraculous sight to miraculous sight on every inhabited planet under view from the thought-crafts.

"I will project myself into a female form," Gutkir continued, "although less strong, they seem the most resilient." Simultaneously millions of leader Tgirams were choosing particular forms of life in which to exist for a period of discovery.

"How much in this planet's conception of time is half a unit of space time?" rapped out Gutkir.

"It is exactly one Earth day," replied Sfim, busily assimilating the planet's information in his thinking bank.

"I wish a random female form to be chosen for me by the random locator," clicked Gutkir, "I will then have increased time to thought-read essential information for survival on this planet."

"Is that a good idea?" tapped Sfim timidly. "Would an intelligent and mentally stable creature not be best — their surroundings would surely prove more useful."

"No," replied Gutkir strongly. "It is my consciousness that occupies their form and I may take that form where I choose — have you not noticed their remarkable mobility?"

Sfim bowed to the more assertive thoughts of Gutkir, carefully screening his own objections. The random locator whirred impressively around Earth.

It was the morning of the Church Bazaar and Miss Marion Hilton was in a very slight panic. Before her on the table of her tiny kitchen lay a mountain of lovingly made fabric-wrapped coat-hangers, crocheted picture frame mats, potholders, teacosies and fringed muffs. There were also crocheted fireside slippers with pompoms, a calico chequebook holder, snowgirl doll socks, circular sachets with eyelet borders and hang loops, various knitted animals and a large pink gingham stuffed pig.

She was adding the final touches to several flower wrist pincushions and wondering if she would be in time to get a good stall in the church hall, without looking too pushy. Snipping off stray threads, she admired her work, piled it neatly in a cardboard box, and put on her hat and coat for the walk along to Westpriors Church.

"I'm going to have to leave you here, Fluffy," she crooned indulgently to her small blue-rinsed poodle, "but I'll be back soon darling." Fluffy snarled unnervingly and slumped on her cushion. Miss Hilton hurried down her front path, pushing the door shut behind her. It didn't quite close.

"One micro unit till projection," warned Sfim. Gutkir turned his thoughts from reading Earth thought patterns. Sfim sensed disturbance — Gutkir clicked quietly, "The thoughts are irrational. These creatures seem to think one thing, but say another. They portray insincere emotions and use predictable speech patterns which do not reflect their true feelings. There is an intense need for communication, but inadequacy and fear in the actual act. These beings seem to be isolated from one another, some to extremes. There is a disturbing amount of hatred on this planet, an amount that our own thought shields could not mask from others."

"Surely a cumulative effect," soothed Sfim, "in individual cases the form will be milder. You will not be isolated like them, as you can still communicate with us."

"True, my friend Sfim," replied Gutkir, "I am fully prepared for projection."

"Signal imminent," interrupted a powerful long-distance thoughtwave.

"Awaiting signal and prepared," they sent back in unison.

Miss Hilton walked sedately along Birch Avenue towards the Church. To some people she nodded, to others she said "Hello", and to a select few she said "A lovely morning, isn't it?".

In actual fact she was oblivious to the rich autumn leaves and crisp air as she crunched along the gravel to the door of the hall. She was thinking about more important things, which stall she would get — and who would be placed on either side of her. God forbid it would be that truly awful Mrs Brown or her henpecked daughter, Jennifer.

"Hello Miss Hilton," beamed the Vicar. He was radiant, much help was arriving and it looked as though it would be a profitable morning. He looked into her box and his smile grew even broader.

"How delightful! And what a lovely pig! Miss Hilton, you must allow us to offer your pig as first prize in the pressed flower calendar competition."

"Certainly." Miss Hilton was gratified — that would be one in the eye for Mrs Brown with her napkin ring holders and knitted animals. She hurried into the hall and made her way towards the stall that she wanted, it was empty. It looked as if everything was going her way.

As she set out her merchandise she smiled around the other ladies. Mrs Wilson was there, as was Miss Shaw and Miss Mills. Miss Mills hurried over.

"Hello Marion! What lovely things — you must have put a lot of work into them. Thankfully my baking only takes me the night before."

"Your sponge cakes look marvellous, Betty," replied Miss Hilton, "you really have excelled yourself this time!" Miss Mills reddened with pleasure.

"Do you think so? Between you and me, your fabric-covered coathangers are the neatest I've seen yet. Far better than Mrs Brown's were last year."

"Talk of the devil," interrupted Miss Hilton quickly, "and she's coming this way."

"Marion! Betty!" Mrs Brown gushed, "how nice to see you! Do you mind if I take this stall next to yours, Marion?"

"Not at all," said Miss Hilton tightly.

"I doubt if it will be big enough," Mrs Brown continued gaily, "I have knitted more than a hundred animals this year. Jennif-er. Bring in the other boxes!"

Miss Hilton cursed her luck as she arranged her work; in sheer bulk it would seem inferior to Mrs Brown's mounds of dreadful animals. Miss Mills went back to her own stall musing over the tastelessness of Miss Hilton's fringed muffs.

Soon villagers of Westpriors milled around the hall picking up their scones and egg-warmers, socks and home-made desk tidies. Miss Hilton smiled around brightly, hoping that Fluffy wasn't getting her own back for her captivity by messing up the kitchen floor. In actual fact, Fluffy had just found that the door wasn't closed, and was making her way determinedly along Birch Avenue.

Suddenly Miss Hilton felt quite queer and had to sit down.

On the given signal Gutkir projected himself to the creature indicated by the random locator. Sfim sent thoughts of encouragement after him.

"My goodness, Miss Hilton has fainted! Get a glass of water!" The ladies of Westpriors Church rallied around their prone friend with advice. Mrs Brown and her daughter lifted her back into her chair.

"She's coming to," Jennifer pointed out. Gutkir opened his new eyes and started in horror. Sfim could feel waves of panic. Leaning over him were the ugliest assortment of Earth's creatures that he had yet seen. At close range the hanging mouths and pouchy faces were truly horrible.

"Are you alright?" said one of them.

"Yes, of course," Gutkir used Miss Hilton's voice admirably, although to the other ladies she seemed to be talking in a lower pitch than normal. "I will be alright, please don't worry." But it was too late, a creature all in black with a white collar was hurrying over. Was this one of their policemen? Gutkir appealed to Sfim and was told it was a Vicar — a man who claimed to be an intermediary between these beings and the unknown power that they were supposed to love. Gutkir felt little love.

"Miss Hilton, you must go home and lie down. We are all deeply distressed that you are unwell — and admire you for coming to help anyway."

"Vicar I am completely recovered now," Gutkir said steadily, "and I must insist that I carry on as normal." Soon the Vicar had retreated, muttering gratefully. Gutkir surveyed the hideous and seemingly useless objects on the stall before him.

"I'll have one of your fringed muffs," said an old lady. Frantically Gutkir contacted Sfim who was identifying the objects with obvious amusement. Sfim directed him and he handed her the muff.

"Thank you!" The old lady handed him the twenty pence requested on the price list and walked off. Gutkir stared after her unbelievingly as she hung the object around her neck and stuck her hands inside it.

Miss Mills nudged Miss Shaw and pointed to the door of the hall.

"Fluffy has come looking for Marion again." Fluffy ran to her owner, but instead of a joyful greeting began to bark wildly and snarl at Miss Hilton. Miss Mills and Miss Shaw looked over in surprise and were even more surprised to see Miss Hilton back away in terror and start to run. She ran, faster than she had ever been seen to run before, out of the hall, slamming the door shut behind her. Fluffy was left trembling and whining in a pile of snowgirl doll socks which had been knocked over by Gutkir in his panic.

"I don't know what's come over Miss Hilton, I really don't," Miss Shaw tutted disapprovingly.

"It's certainly very strange," agreed Miss Wilson, who was passing.

Gutkir stood trembling outside the church. A totally unexpected life form had confronted him fiercely and he had used his new human mobility for such an emergency. Sfim was trying to get through to him, but Gutkir shielded himself temporarily from messages. He needed some time to recover.

He walked along Birch Avenue using the standard "Good Morning" to those who seemed to recognise him. Some seemed to look surprised, others disappointed at this greeting. He was looking forward to reading the minds of these creatures — which he hadn't been able to do in the enclosed space of the Church Hall. A lady who seemed to know his form approached.

"Hello Miss Hilton! I thought that you were at the Church Bazaar."

Her mind reflected genuine surprise.

"I was, but I decided to get some fresh air as I felt unwell," he replied.

"Oh dear! I hope it is nothing serious!" Gutkir was surprised to feel satisfaction rather than concern coming from the mind of the lady.

"I'm really alright," Gutkir said. "Where are you going?"

"To visit my sister — you know Pat." She was lying. Gutkir dug deeper in her mind. Amid excited, guilty emotions he could see a man, much younger than she was. He could not understand why she was lying, until he saw a picture of another man — obviously her life partner — in her mind.

The lady walked on and Gutkir tried to control the feeling of nausea that was coming over him — a human equivalent of extreme Tgiram distaste. He dropped his thought shields.

"Gutkir!" tapped out Sfim urgently. "We've been ordered to withdraw immediately, project yourself back to the thought-craft!"

He did not need a second bidding. Back on the craft he looked down and saw Miss Hilton start slightly, look a bit confused, and then head resolutely back towards the Church Bazaar.

On Tgir every thought-craft was being destroyed. One thought, of relief, rose around the planet. Every craft leader had from every planet involuntarily sent powerful thoughtwaves of disgust back to Tgir. Tgir seemed to be the only planet where the inhabitants communicated freely — conditions on the planets they had visited bred evil. Gutkir had experienced this evil only in mild form, but many others were undergoing treatment for shock.

Back in the Church Hall Mrs Wilson came up to Miss Hilton's stall.

"I do hope you're feeling better, Marion," she began, but Miss Hilton looked at her strangely.

"No you dont."

THE CHINA FACED DOLL

Wilma Murray

"Is it Sunday?"

The wire hairbrush is tugging and pulling at unruly red curly hair, jerking the child's head back at each stroke in time with her mother's internal rhythm of annoyance.

"No. It's not. Now stand still. Meg? Do you hear me?" She reinforces her question with a quick flick of the brush against the child's backside. She separates hair, combs and pleats it in the fashion of the times and anchors the last sprialling tendrils with hairgrips. "You've got hair just like your Dad's. Now, let me look at you."

The child turns round to face her mother's critical eyes.

"Is Dad coming home on leave? Is that why I'm getting all dressed up?" The mother shakes her head.

"You'll do," she says.

"Where am I going then?"

"Miss Mabel wants to take you out. Jessie's coming up for you. Now stay clean till she comes. Promise?"

"Promise. Why doesn't Miss Marjory take Miss Mabel up here for me herself?"

"Huh! You've got a lot to learn, Meg."

"I don't like Jessie. She smells."

The mother looks sharply at the child, then away.

"That's the smell of hard work. And don't you ever forget it."

"Miss Mabel always smells nice."

"Yes, well. So might Jessie, if she never had to do a hand's turn.

Keep a look out for her now, and remember what I said about keeping clean."

From the window of the cottage, Meg has a view of the steep curved drive lined with great bushes of rhododendrons, almost as tall as trees and solemn green now after their extravagant spring showing.

"R-H-O-D-O-D-E-N-D-R-O-N." Meg spells the word to herself softly.

"I can spell rhododendron. It's the longest word in the world, isn't it?"

"No."

"Yes it is! Miss Marjory said so."

"No she didn't."

"Well . . ." Meg turns back to the window. All spring, she has watched the bees working among the rhododendron flowers, wriggling their fat furry backsides into the bells and making the bushes hum. They are gone now.

"Do you think Miss Mabel will let me ride Brindy again?"

"Brindy's lame."

"Oh, my poor Brindy. What happened?"

"He's not your Brindy, and I don't know what happened."

"But I get to ride him. I'm the only one who gets to."

"Mm. Well, not today."

'Maybe we'll go up to the gardens, then. I really like that best of all."

The mother sighs. "Maybe." She comes up to the window, looking out over the child's shoulder, wiping floury hands on a rough towel apron she wears fastened over her usual one on baking day. "Here she comes. Go on and meet her. Save her the last of the hill. Be good now. And don't come back with your pockets full of rabbits' dirt like last time."

Meg runs from the house eagerly to meet Jessie struggling up the hill.

"Good lass. I'm just about puffed out, so I am." She tries to take Meg's hand, but the child wriggles away and runs on ahead, stopping now and then to watch her shadow pirouette in the stiff blue Sunday dress.

"Who's a pretty girl today, then?"

"I am."

The ladies are waiting by the front steps of the Hall, two lean women in dull tweeds and knitted stockings, the elder in a wheelchair, the younger holding its cane handle. They are smiling. Miss Mabel leans forward in the chair as Meg comes up to them.

"Ah, there you are, Margaret. How pretty you look today. Come and kiss me." Miss Mabel holds out her arms and Meg runs into them, hugging the bony shoulders and kissing the wrinkled cheek below the ear, just where the soft grey hair sweeps back to a bun.

"Thank you, Jessie, that will be all. Come, Marjory. To the gardens, I think. Would you like that, Margaret?"

"Oh, yes. Please."

The ladies watch with indulgent smiles as Meg skips on ahead, up the path through the park which leads to the walled gardens.

"Now. Let's see what you can remember from last time, Margaret. Tell me the names of the trees, please."

Meg smiles and repeats clearly the name of each tree they pass; oak and beech, lime and sycamore, yew, holly and gean.

"Very good! And what is that one there?" Miss Mabel points to the large unusual tree standing by itself near the iron door in the garden wall.

"A monkey puzzle."

"Yes. What a clever little girl! You see, Marjory? She remembers everything we teach her. She really does."

The wrought-iron door opens on a calendar garden, complete with a sundial, bird baths and stone cherubs. The scent is rich and heady; seemingly contained by the high ivy-covered walls; warm, soft scents of lavender, honeysuckle and roses and, above that, the high note of the tang of tiger lilies. They progress very slowly along the neat paths, touching and looking, Miss Mabel's chair crunching over the fine gravel and sticking now and then in its soft depth.

"Run and see if you can find Thomson, Margaret. Tell him I want to speak to him."

Meg finds the old gardener weeding in the kitchen garden, at the far end, near the greenhouse wall. She calls and waves and he turns from his work to greet her.

"Miss Mabel sent me to get you."

"Oh she did, did she? Are you the new skivvy, then?"

Thomson rises slowly and unties the canvas patches from his knees, knocking them free of dirt against his trousers. He kicks each boot against the base of a stone cherub at the corner of the path. He lifts his cap, rakes a hand through his hair, then replaces the cap. It has left a tidemark on his forehead, white and soft above, brown and leathery below.

"Well now, we'd better go, then. What are you up to today?"

"Miss Mabel is taking me round the gardens. Maybe I'll get some flowers to take home for Mam."

"Maybe. I wouldn't count on it, though."

"She sometimes gives me flowers I can tell the names of. I've learned a lot of the names now. Would you like to hear me?"

"Go on then."

As they walk, Meg rattles off the names breathlessly, in a jumbled string of sounds made meaningless by speed.

Thomson grins at her, but sets his face to rights as they approach the ladies.

"There you are, Thomson. The garden seems to be thriving. There are, however, some climbers in need of attention on the south wall. And the delphiniums require staking."

"Yes, Ma'am."

"Now. About flowers for the Hall. We have guests coming this weekend. We will need roses for the rose bowls and three bouquets for the bedrooms. Can we manage that?"

"Yes, Ma'am."

"Thank you, Thomson. Oh, how far along are the strawberries?"

"I put down the first picking for the table this morning."

"Splendid. Come, Marjory. Let's be getting along. Margaret will be getting bored."

The little procession moves on towards the central fountain, which no longer works, its cherubs frozen in the act of blowing bubbles. One cherub has lost its nose, another a hand. Margaret jumps up and scrambles over the lip of the wide stone basin, balancing on the edge, face downwards.

"It's still there." The cherub's severed hand lies palm upwards at the bottom of the basin. Meg had put a penny in it a long time ago. As she slips down from the fountain, scraping her tummy, her dress bunches up in a roll over her white knickers.

"Margaret! Your dress!" Miss Marjory hurries to set it to rights, smoothing the dress back down to cover her legs.

"Come and see what I have brought you today." Miss Marjory takes her hand and leads her back to the garden seat. From a pocket of her suit she produces a small leather-bound book.

"Is it another book of poems?"

"No. This is a drawing book. See, there are empty pages opposite the drawings for you to copy."

Meg takes the book and flips through the pages filled with perfect line drawings of horses, dogs, trees and flowers.

"Don't you like it?"

"It looks difficult."

'But you must try. Then one day you will be able to draw, like we do."

"Oh, but I'd never be able to draw like you, Miss Mabel."

Miss Mabel laughs. "Not right away. But if you practise, someday you will. Will you try? For me?"

"All right."

"Good girl. Now. What about the poem you've been learning for our Sunday School concert? Can you say it all yet?"

"Oh yes."

"Good. Let's hear it. Miss Marjory and I will be your audience."

"What? Oh . . . I mean, pardon?"

"Audience. People who listen to you recite. Off you go, then."

Without prompting, Meg goes to stand above them on the steps of the fountain and in her sing-song voice recites.

" 'I Don't Like Beetles' by Rose Fyleman.

I don't like beetles, tho' I'm sure they're very good,
I don't like porridge, tho' my Nannie says I should,
I don't like the cistern in the attic where I play,
And the funny noise the bath makes when the water runs away.

I don't like the feeling when my gloves are made of silk,
And that dreadful slimy skinny stuff on top of hot milk,
I don't like tigers, not even in a book,
And I know it's very naughty, but I DON'T LIKE COOK !"

Her audience claps in appreciation and Meg claps with them.

"There! Now you will have a special present. Won't she, Marjory?"

"Oh, yes. We looked out something special for you."

"Tell me what it is! Please! Please!" Meg dances and jumps, her rising chant exciting the doves in the nearby dovecote into a flapping protest.

"Now, Margaret. Patience. It is to be a surprise. Marjory, take her to the rose garden while I rest. She can run about on the grass there. Teach her the names of the roses today."

The tall faded woman in brown tweeds and the small vivid child in the blue dress make daisy chains, smell the roses and play hide and seek among the high shelter hedges. They squeal and laugh as they catch each other. Heat rises from the grass with the pungent tonic smell of summer.

"Oh, stop. Stop! I'm exhausted. It's so hot." Miss Marjory tucks some strands of hair back into her bun and examines a shoe for a stone.

"Don't your legs get very hot?"

"Yes, they do."

"Why don't you take off your stockings? That's what Mam does when it's hot."

"We must be going now. It's almost time for tea."

They return by a different path through the woods, skirting the high-hedged drying green before the Hall comes into view. Here and there, trees are circled with low fences, protecting tiny gravestones with the names of generations of pet dogs. It is cool in the sun-speckled shade, cool and smelling of damp and warm pine resin. A red squirrel darts through the high branches of an old beech and they pause, perfectly still, hardly breathing as it stops to watch them, poised in readiness for acrobatic flight.

Back at the Hall, Jessie is setting afternoon tea on a small table under the chestnut tree on the front lawn. The Shetland ponies stroll into view and right up to the wall, curious and on the lookout for attention and titbits. Meg runs off to stroke their noses, climbing up to reach them.

"Where's Brindy? Mam said he was lame." She calls back to the sisters who exchange looks.

"What happened to him?" Meg persists.

"He caught a leg in a rabbit hole. Now, what about that special present? Jessie, fetch the D-O-L-L from the . . ."

"A doll! Ooh, a doll!" Meg runs up to Miss Mabel and hugs her then repeats the performance with Miss Marjory.

"Yes. A doll for a very clever little girl. It was my doll a long, long time ago. I want you to have it now. You are my little girl, aren't you?" Marjory holds the excited child close to her, gently containing, for a moment, the bundle of vitality within her grasp.

The doll is a little faded, but still beautiful, dressed in many layers of cream shantung and lace. The face is made of china, with painted cheeks and a pretty smile. The eyes are large and blue. As Meg takes it, her own eyes are wide with joy.

"You can run along now, Margaret. Jessie, will you see to it? You can tell her mother she was a very good girl."

"Thank you, Miss Mabel. Thank you, Miss Marjory. I've had a lovely day."

"Don't forget this." Miss Marjory hands her the drawing book.

Meg is solemn and quiet on the way back, hugging the doll and the little book very tightly.

"You're a lucky girl. Those two have taken a right shine to you, you know that? Never had any of their own, of course."

Meg is not listening.

"They wanted to watch you being born, you know. Your Mam was ever so glad you were born at night. She wouldn't have known what excuse to make if you'd come during the day."

Meg is frowning, part of her already shut away. "Do you think Mam will let me keep it?"

"Ah, well. That's not for me to say. She doesn't like you getting spoiled, you know."

The sight of the doll triggers her mother's anger.

"It's far too good for you to play with. What were they thinking about, giving you that? We'll put it away somewhere safe."

"Mam!" Meg clutches the doll tight, refusing to let her mother touch it.

"I don't know. You come back here every time with your head full of their nonsense. And I'm the one who has to suffer it. Poetry and all that fancy stuff. And what's that you've got there?" She points at the book on the table.

"A drawing book. For me."

"Well. Just look at it. What on earth do you think you'll be able to do with that?"

"I'm going to learn to draw, like Miss Mabel."

"Miss Mabel. Miss Mabel. Look, missy. I know all about your precious Miss Mabel. Don't think I don't. No presents for me all those years, getting up at quarter to six, blackleading grates and carrying coal scuttles . . ."

"I don't care! I don't care! I like Miss Mabel. And Miss Marjory. I like them more than I like . . ."

The last word is strangled. The tears of anger and hurt brimming up in her eyes are spilled by her mother's sudden slap.

Hiccuping with sobs, Meg runs from the house and across the yard to the stables, still clutching her prize.

"I'll keep you safe. I'll hide you. I will."

The hay loft above the stable stalls is her secret place, full of soft sweet hay. From across the yard, she can hear her mother call her but she does not answer.

"You're so pretty. Like the pictures in Miss Mabel's books. What will I call you? I'll call you . . ."

Voices in the stable below distract her from her play, a man's voice and Miss Mabel's. By crawling to the edge of the loft, she can see down. They are leading a pony in. Brindy.

Miss Marjory braces the wheelchair with her body. Her face is turned away, her eyes screwed shut. But still the chair bucks with the gun's recoil. The indecent noise is stunningly loud in the confined space. Meg's hands are clamped over her ears and her mouth is open on a suffocated scream.

"Cover him." The groom draws sacking over the head of the dead pony.

THE CHINA FACED DOLL

"Have him buried. Today. Now leave us." The groom takes the gun she holds out to him.

Miss Marjory strokes the round flank of the pony. Meg can hear her mother calling, nearer now and urgent. She mouths a call, but her voice does not come.

"Come, Marjory." When they have gone, Meg struggles to get down the ladder and the china faced doll smiles her pretty smile in the warm soft hay of the loft.

"Mam! Mam! Mam!"

NOTES ON CONTRIBUTORS

JOYCE BEGG is a Glasgow writer. After university she taught briefly, and is now a housewife and mother. Her stories have appeared in several magazines including *Scottish Field* and *Scottish Review* and have been broadcast on radio.

SHEENA BLACKHALL lives in Aberdeen. Having resigned from teaching to raise a family, she continues her writing from home. Her work has appeared in *Edinburgh Review, Leopard, Life and Work, Deeside Field Club* and *Aberdeen Press and Journal*. She has also published *The Cyard's Kist* (Rainbow Books), a collection of poetry. Her poems have been broadcast on radio.

MOIRA BURGESS published her novel, *The Day Before Tomorrow* (Collins), while working as a librarian. She graduated from Strathclyde University with a thesis on the Glasgow novel, and after concentrating on marriage and motherhood has returned to writing seriously. She was awarded a Scottish Arts Council Bursary in 1982. She is co-editor of *Streets of Stone* (Salamander Press), an anthology of Scottish short stories, and her own stories are included in *New Writing Scotland 2* and *3* (Association for Scottish Literary Studies) and *Scottish Short Stories 1985* (Collins).

SUSAN CAMPBELL was brought up in the Highlands and Skye, and now lives in Glasgow. She graduated from Glasgow University last year with an English and Psychology degree and is currently writing short stories and film scripts. She is the co-author of a script, *The Stranger*, which is being produced this year with the Scottish Film Council. One of her stories has appeared in *Short Story Monthly*.

ELIZABETH CASE has published a romantic suspense novel, *The House That Lochinvar Built*, and short stories in various women's magazines including *Woman's Realm* and *Woman's Weekly*. She has lived most of her life in Troon and is past president of Ayr Writers' Club.

ANNE DOWNIE is a professional actress and writer living in Glasgow. Her plays, *Cracked, De Profundis* and *Retribution*, have been performed in Scotland. She is working on two play commissions and acting with Theatre About Glasgow, the Citizens Theatre touring company. She has two children.

IRIS DOYLE studied at the Reid Kerr College and the Glasgow School of Art before moving north to Caithness a few years ago. She is working on a novel. *The Letter* is her first publication.

NOTES ON CONTRIBUTORS

ROSEMARY MACKAY is an Aberdonian writer. An arts graduate, she has retired from school-teaching twice. She began writing short stories a few years ago and recently started on a novella. *Lunch* is her first publication.

MARY McCABE was born and bred in Glasgow where she works as a careers officer. She has published short stories in *Cencrastus* and *Chapman* and a children's story book *Die zauberhafte Reise* (Schneider), translated and published in Germany. Several of her radio plays have been broadcast in Germany.

LINDA McCANN worked for several years before beginning her current studies at Glasgow University. *The Golfer* is her first publication.

LINDA McLEAN lives in Bishopton. She and her husband have a three-year-old daughter and are expecting another child soon. *I Find It All A Little Bit Frightening* is her first publication.

ELLEN McMILLAN works as a receptionist in Glasgow and has written for pleasure since primary school. *For Better Or Else* is her first publication.

JANE MORRIS has contributed articles to various women's magazines and writes a regular medical column in *Cosmopolitan*. Born in Birmingham, she studied English and Medicine at Cambridge University and now lives in Edinburgh with her husband.

WILMA MURRAY is a lecturer in the Geography Department of the Aberdeen College of Education. She started writing seriously three years ago, since when her stories have been published in *New Edinburgh Review, Glasgow Magazine, The New Writer, Scotsman Magazine, Scottish Review* and *New Writing Scotland*.

AGNES OWENS was born in Milngavie and now lives in Balloch. Her first novel, *Gentlemen of the West* (Polygon) was published in 1984 and received a book award from the Scottish Arts Council; she is now working on its sequel. A selection of her stories will be appearing with those of James Kelman and Alasdair Gray in *Lean Tales* (Cape).

JOY PITMAN has worked as a teacher of English and creative writing, an archivist, a mother, a publisher (she is a founder member of Stramullion) and administrator. Her poems have appeared in *Hens in the Hay* (Stramullion), *Spare Rib, Radical Scotland* and *Chapman*. She has recently completed her first novel.

NOTES ON CONTRIBUTORS

DILYS ROSE was brought up in Glasgow, and came to Edinburgh to study English Literature and Philosophy. She has been involved with Women Live in Scotland and part of the editorial team of *Radical Scotland*. Her stories and poems have appeared in *Lines Review, The Honest Ulsterman, Glasgow Magazine, Radical Scotland* and *Graffiti*.

JENNIFER RUSSELL was born and raised in Glasgow and is studying English and Psychology at Glasgow University. *The Evil Planets* is her first publication.

MORELLE SMITH lives in the Borders with her husband and two children. Two volumes of her poetry, *The Star Reaper* (Grade One Press) and *The Long Fields* (Sunbow Press), have been published, and her poems and stories have appeared in *Chapman* and *Graffiti*. She studies astrology and has contributed articles to *The Edinburgh Astrologer*.

WENDY STEWART was born in Edinburgh and now works as a nurse in London where she is involved with healthcare politics and trade union activities. Her fiction and poetry have appeared in *City Limits, Bananas, Spare Rib* and *The Looker*, and her articles and essays in *The Scotsman, Glasgow Herald, Militant, Socialist Worker* and *Socialist Scotland*.

JANE STRUTH developed an interest in poetry at Hamilton College which led her to write children's and, more recently, adult short stories. She completed an Open University arts degree while looking after her four young children. *The Tea-Room* is her first publication.

JANETTE WALKINSHAW lives a self-sufficient life on a smallholding in Renfrewshire with her husband and a herd of goats. She has published a short story in *Clanjamfrie* (Polygon).

RHIANNON WILLIAMS lives in Paisley. After leaving school she spent a year in Frankfurt am Main involved in Green politics and teaching English. She is now studying English at Cambridge University and is involved in the Pornography is Violence Against Women campaign. *Thinking About Marriage* is her first publication.